G000057160

sacred cow

. . . .

sacred cow

....

diamela eltit

translated by amanda hopkinson

Library of Congress Catalog Card Number: 93-87663

A complete catalogue record for this book can be obtained
from the British Library on request

The right of Diamela Eltit to be identified as the author of
this work has been asserted by her in accordance with the
Copyright, Designs and Patents Act 1988

First published in Spanish in 1991 as *Vaca Sagrada*
by Grupo Editorial Planeta, Santiago

Copyright © 1991 Grupo Editorial Planeta
Translation © 1995 Amanda Hopkinson

This edition first published in 1995 by
Serpent's Tail, 4 Blackstock Mews, London N4
and 180 Varick Street, 10th floor, New York, NY 10014

Set in 10.5 pt Caslon by CentraCet Ltd, Cambridge
Printed in Finland by Werner Söderström Oy

sacred cow

....

one

....

I sleep, I dream, I lie a lot. The birdlike shape has vanished. What is the vanished shape? Wherever I go, a terrifying eye follows me, preventing me from working. I am incapable of understanding a world. I am skilful with only a part of me, with only the part of a part; I can scarcely see the narrow way in to the sex of the part. A demand from hell forces my thoughts towards twisted shapes, plagued by mutilations. I dream, I bleed a lot. They have destroyed my powerful flight of birds and its fine display over the city. After so much effort, I have lost the train of reason, of names, and all my stories are unravelling. I bleed, lie a lot. Now, barely warmed by a glass of wine, I wonder – in what state of collapse will I have to outlast the harshness of winter?

two

....

discovery

I was in mid-crisis when I met Manuel. For some time I'd been struggling between euphoria and melancholia, both equally impossible to alleviate. I was consumed by elusive desires and driven by insecurity towards a shattering destiny. I'd already acquired the habit of constant lying. Although I always loathed it, I seemed compelled despite myself: given the slightest encouragement I'd launch into some fabrication that inevitably led to endless problems since I frequently forgot what I'd said, and more than once was brought up short, faced by my own contradictions.

It was perhaps this craziness that made me court situations of extreme risk. I hung around in bars, where the wine taught me that the quality of words counted for little, since death lay hidden at the bottom of the glass.

Manuel watched over me. It seemed as though his sole function was to push me into situations that put me to sleep at the least appropriate moment. One evening I woke in the toilet of a bar, lying on the floor covered in my own vomit. Out of my mind, the shapes of things were confused, the walls and ceiling began to revolve in ever larger blurred circles, while Manuel struggled to bring me back to a reality I found the more unbearable whenever I opened my eyes.

He knew about my lies and didn't seem to care. I respected him for this and got used to a kind of complicity. It wasn't an understanding exactly in the sense of a pact; more like a game we'd made up to avoid confronting our dilemma, each of us alone.

. . . .

Manuel came from the South and continually talked about the place. City-dweller that I was, his obsession felt foreign to me. I've always detested unnecessary attachment to places and particularly nostalgic attachment. I'd already decided to avoid any kind of personal involvement. I wasn't too bothered about sex, which seemed to me little more than an excessive if gratifying ritual. Perhaps I was just making light of hidden terrors, but I didn't much trust the mingling of bodies – it had certainly never given me any sensation beyond what I'd already experienced on my own.

Manuel was tolerant of my habits and didn't demand passion. In fact he himself seemed to have discarded the idea of constant sexual activity and we frequently discussed this surprising coincidence. He only came to life when he discussed the South, the South. The South was his greatest gift and from his words I learned about rowdy houses drenched by rains, about erupting nature, about rocks embracing the sea. Pucatrihue was his passion. He said that one day in Pucatrihue we would catch up with the light.

. . . .

I taught him wine's true value. I introduced him into the intense camaraderie of wine and let him weave his personal stories of the South from its dark liquid reflections. Manuel was lying. He'd migrated from the South because he hated it, but in denouncing it he was denouncing me and I needed his confirmation of all my fantasies. Pucatrihue was hell. Its angry seas devoured human bodies, ghostly faces leered from its twisted trees. We went along with all this horror, submitted without resistance, thus forming a pact, based on compromises that concealed the weight of our lies.

Manuel had brought his wife with him from the South. Barely out of his teens he had married a strangely passive girl. She didn't interest me in the least. It only took Manuel's brief description of the magnitude of their problems to rid me of any curiosity about this young woman who wandered through the city in search of an explanation for the abrupt loss of his affection and her suspicions of this foreign territory.

At one stage she sought me out to arrange a meeting, and I had no alternative but to turn up as we'd agreed, to clarify the reasons for their separation. I agreed to go at Manuel's insistence, despite my previous practice of always avoiding such encounters. When Marta arrived, I was thrown by an unexpected detail: one of her eyes was very obviously filmed over. I was so struck by this that I stared longer than I should. She seemed upset by my scrutiny and it was not until I noticed her wry smile that I looked away and concentrated on what she was saying.

The girl spoke without pausing. Bereft at her loss of Manuel, she blamed the chaos of the city for his unexpected change of heart. Timidly, she outlined her notion that possibly he and I were planning a new future together. I found myself moved by her words, but my fondness for lies made me invent a love affair we'd never had. Distressed by the tragedy I'd invented, I found myself immersed in guilt that wasn't really mine and although I understood the suffering of the weeping woman, I couldn't help adding to her anguish by embellishing the details, the promises, the reconciliations of this nonexistent affair.

Suddenly she decided to leave. We parted with a degree of empathy, and as I walked home I wondered what she was looking for, this Southern girl with the clouded eye. I found no better answer than fear. Fear – though we didn't know it yet – was silently and irrevocably eating into us.

············

Manuel was waiting for me at the door of my house. From a way off I could just make him out leaning against the wall. He wasn't beautiful, but his features possessed an elegant harmony. There was something rather theatrical about him, as if the way he moved was the result of long practice. When I drew near to him I saw that he was agitated and, for the first time, thought that perhaps Marta meant a lot to him. He immediately demanded to know the outcome of our meeting and I decided that to protect myself I would not tell him what had happened. I found his evident anxiety tiresome and irritating, so without much thought I told him that I hadn't kept our appointment – that I'd decided it was none of my business and that the two of them had better sort out their own problems.

'Fucking bitch,' he answered.

As the evening wore on, our dialogue reflected more and more the acidity of the wine. Wounded and nagged by doubts, I gave him an intimate run-down on Sergio.

Knowing how Manuel loathed Sergio, I latched on to the name and with the greatest of ease found myself inventing an almost mythical encounter on some street corner charged with emotion.

We drank through the night and inevitably got drunk. As usual when I was upset, I cried at the memory of some grief suffered years before. Manuel finished up by talking about Marta, but nothing he said bore any relation to the girl I had just met a few hours earlier. Although I was wrapped up in my own thoughts, I think I understood him to say that she was now a memory, and that he had consigned her and his desire for her to history.

We went back to his room and we coupled with outlandish passion. His body grew big and part of my need was exorcised. I felt him coming, felt his rhythmic moving on me as he said, 'Fucking bitch. You're a fucking bitch.'

'I'm not, I'm not, I'm not,' I murmured.

We reached our climax together – astonishingly we collapsed together.

············

A profound change had taken place in our bodies. Quite unexpectedly we found new kinds of intimacy. I learnt that I could use Manuel's body in ways I had never imagined. I gave myself up to the subtleties of his skin, to the erogenous zones of his flesh. Ah such nights, such afternoons – through flux and reflux we went on to reach the all-embracing astonishment of an instant. Manuel always naked. Moaning naked at my side, begging me to excite him further. To remember his hands, his tongue, his saliva, his spilled juices, his energy encouraged by the wine. For months I managed to be simply a body conducting its functions, a body intensified by the archaic language used to vilify it.

We followed every whim, submitting ourselves to an apprenticeship that became more and more inventive. On heat, overheated, nothing could restrain us. Not even my blood. I stood upright with my legs apart and my blood ran down over Manuel: a relentless image. We looked at the red stains on his body, on the sheets – the blood streaming from the slit between my legs. Manuel begged me to taint him with my blood. And I surrendered it to him: fully erect he explored me to elicit and enjoy the viscous liquid. Manuel too seemed himself to be bleeding from an incurable wound running the full length of his body. It was in the blood that we reached the very epicentre of our sexual storm, wrecked on the menacing floods that rocked our deranged senses.

We never spoke of the blood. We simply awaited the commotion it produced in our bodies. Conceived in blood, our words became murderous. As pleasure overtook us, speech incited us to enact lethal passions when pleasure overwhelmed us – the wound, my wound, laceration, death, entrails. Afterwards we lay still, watching how the blood dried and hardened on our bodies. My blood was that power. Although we pretended that the privilege was shared, with one part of my mind I began to resent the energy it took to construct, bit by bit, the perfection of each individual scenario.

. . . .

Trust developed between us until we reached a complete understanding. Without needing to go into things deeply, we reached the same conclusions about people. At this time I was not interested in anyone in particular and I thought that a gift for friendship, or even simple conversation, only led to problems. Manuel saw things differently. He was more talkative, more enthusiastic, he hung around in corridors, on the lookout for leads, trying out countless friendships. This was the side of him that most worried me since it continually exposed him to destruction.

It was basically this annoying habit that set up an imperceptible rift between us. The night he turned up in the bar with a girl who never stopped talking, I realised I had reached my limit. The girl was noisy, not too bright, and made a scene that Manuel couldn't stop, even though he knew that I always found such behaviour embarrassing – just as I find all vulgarity embarrassing. The woman was living a day by day existence, not getting up till evening in order to enjoy what she called 'night life'. When I heard that expression I thought I'd be sick, but I had to carry on with an effort at self-control.

I refused to take part in this farce and quite openly disassociated myself from the others. Feeling awkward, I was gazing into space when I met the look of someone at the next table. It took only a moment to recognise Sergio. I had an instant desire to leave the place and let the night carry on without my assistance.

I could see here a dangerous group: its habits too complex, its outward appearance quite perfect. But the night had already lowered my defences and I could do nothing against it. I could easily recognise how risky Sergio's sickly nostalgia could be. And I already knew that this man was going to latch on to me as if I were the only living thing in a place of death. But what I never could have guessed was that my own gaze would remain inviting, pleading for its own destruction.

. . . .

Sergio got up from his table and came straight over to us. I thought he was going to sit down at our table, but he simply leaned over to speak to me then walked off out of the bar. Manuel was furious and abruptly tried to get rid of the girl so we could be on our own. Without really grasping what was going on, she turned on us until she finally had to admit defeat and leave us to ourselves.

Manuel was adept at facing insults and abuse, though the girl didn't know this. To tell the truth few people were aware of this magnificent quality of his. Behind his geniality there lay a violent being ready to attack on the instant, which he would do using the element of surprise to ambush the other into complete surrender.

He wanted to know why Sergio had come up to me. He started to imagine signals, gestures I might have made to attract the man's attention. I realised that he was enjoying himself and I let him. I think I even encouraged his version of events since I felt weak that night and needed to feel someone antagonising me to keep control of my thoughts.

'Warm my heart,' he murmured, repeating the phrase Sergio had said to me when he leaned over to brush my cheek with his lips. Manuel could not have heard the words; they were scarcely even whispered so there was not the remotest possibility that he could have caught them. I felt enmeshed in an extraordinary coincidence and started looking this way and that at this sentence which linked us. My heart beat exceptionally slowly, making me very anxious. My heart is at the centre of my life and always has been. Secretly I have always been terrified by the feebleness of my heartbeat. Although I know now that this is a somewhat exaggerated concern, the truth is that it has been a lifelong obsession.

It is on the bodily plane that I am most vulnerable, it's my weakest point. So that the demand both men were making of me was the same as drives all my actions, a claim I would never have been capable of formulating so clearly for myself. My heartbeats are so far apart – and I feel as though I have been dragging this defect around since birth. But at this stage I still believed that there was nothing that was irreversible and when I heard both men taking on my own injunction, I took it as a sign of a bodily cure, as an act of love for my body.

Later, as we were wandering through the city – I should say that tension in the city was already extreme – Manuel announced that he was going back to the South. Although this news upset me, I realised that the distance between us would allow me to unwind. I thought that by getting away from Manuel I would rediscover a part of myself I had lost. I explained all this to him, and he in turn told me that he was going back to the South to try to overcome his long aversion to the landscape. As we said goodbye, a sudden feeling of abandonment made me exclaim despite myself, 'You don't love me'.

The night wore on and I parted from him on a street corner that to this day lives on in my memory as enemy territory.

············

It was then that Sergio came back to loo̲
knew full well that he was the one person
was futilely attempting not to cross. And it ̲
an aura of death finally settled on the city. M̲
no attempt to get in touch until I learned ̲that he had
been detained in the South along with his whole family.
Even as I feared his assassination, I recognised that I was
trying not to think about such danger. I have a strong
inclination to drown in any upheaval, and the disorder
marking that whole period left me no alternative.

Disarmed, confused, I left my own story behind to
resume my apprenticeship to the map of the city, the
city's bodies, the city's features. The obsession with my
existence lost all its attraction. In my agitated state of
mind, my fears focused on the danger from without, the
cold without, the nights, the obvious dangers of the
nights. With trepidation, Sergio and I went back to the
bars to remind ourselves of the solace that wine can
bring. We would sit for hours at some slightly hidden
table, waiting expectantly to catch sight of people we
knew. I forced myself to feel continually seduced since
I had to cling to something in order to efface the
unleashed perversity of those times.

three

....

arrival

She asked the neighbour to take her to Francisca's house as quickly as possible. The neighbour tried to dissuade her saying that there were traffic restrictions in force in the city. But she insisted, convinced by the certainty that this was an emergency. She wanted to go, she needed to confirm with her own eyes what was going on. The neighbour didn't utter a word to her during the journey, and his repugnance for the trip could be measured by the speed at which he took it. Once outside the house, he asked if he should wait for her, but she said no, she'd be spending the night there.

She saw that the front door was open. 'How could they have left the door open?' she thought, and, terrified that her worst fears were about to be realised, she went into the house. In the darkness of the corridor someone was calling her, and Francisca's voice led her through the gloom. 'It seems as though she has deliberately set up this scene', she thought. 'It seems as though she has set this scene up for herself and that I am simply here as her witness.'

As she went into the bedroom, Francisca switched on the light. What she saw, how she saw it, filled her with panic. Not with pity or revulsion, but with panic. Francisca was lying naked on her bed and her face was one huge bruise surrounded by dried blood. 'I have to get out of here,' she thought; but went to sit on the edge of the bed. She found herself looking at one eye closed by the swelling and the skin round it slowly colouring a deep spreading purple. 'I want to get out,' she thought again, quite unable to speak as she pulled the sheet up over the body.

She didn't want to know what she already knew, she had no desire to go into the promiscuity of detail, she didn't want to know anything whatsoever. Suddenly she felt very ill and on an uncontrollable impulse announced:

'I'm off. I've got to get out of here.'

Francisca, Francisca's obliterated face, gave an indication of pain and her hand slid out from between the sheets. She didn't speak; she didn't even whisper. She just lay on her side, staring at her and tightly clutching her hand. She got the feeling that Francisca had made her come at this moment of extreme danger simply for this – to sense, despite the damaged vision in one eye, that someone was still there to hold her hand.

She decided she should stay, wait with her until morning, get to learn all the details, and – worst of all – respond to the predictable words suffused with the familiar rage. 'I don't know what to do,' she thought. 'I don't know what more I can do for her.' She thought back to that other Francisca, the one that had been there before, but she failed to reconcile the two images. 'What happened?' she asked herself. 'How could she have come to this?' But at that very moment, Francisca let out something like a groan and she cut short her thoughts to stroke her wounded face.

'It'll soon get better,' she said.

She sounded like a mother talking to her little daughter who has fallen over or suddenly got earache. She was speaking as if to a child, wanting to protect her from the sordid darkness, the silence of the street, the vast loneliness that surrounded them.

'How can I help you?' she wondered as she bent to see how severe the wounds were. 'She has been beaten,' she thought, 'but there are no broken bones.'

She whispered her name; Francisca replied with hers and the effort caused a thin trickle of blood to dribble from the corner of her mouth. She leaned over to hear what she was saying.

'It was my fault,' said Francisca. 'This time it was entirely my fault.'

four

....

the enigma of the city

There is no way to describe in detail what those days were like, because days like those cannot be contained in words. There is no earthly way of describing how all the signs began to disintegrate. It was both subtle and violent. It was all inside my head, and at the same time it was only out in the world. Something seemed to be irradiating everything, as if a single mind had gone raving mad and was lashing out senselessly. Death took hold in the least expected places, death remained everywhere invisible.

It is pointless to be exact now about things that then I couldn't grasp. In truth, the measure of what was going on was only in the air and I still maintain that the human voice changes when reality shifts to the margins. I don't want to go into that. Though perhaps if I really tried I could pinpoint the onset of my fear. But I'm not going to. As I've already said, I don't want to go into it. I can't. I have forgotten exactly what happened and can only just bring back images, bits of images, words without images. A command, a flight, a shout, the sound of war, a pecking, a woman's groans. Not even these.

I can't remember what dramas might have taken shape before my very eyes. Sergio turned up in the bar and told me that Manuel had been detained in the South

along with all his family. As he said it, I remembered his
face and began to fantasise: we were in a bar, making
love leaning against the wall of the toilet and I was about
to come together with him. How badly I wanted Manuel
that day! My body was on fire and its only hope of
pleasure was confined in some secret place in the South.

············

My imagination ran riot. Without my willing it, I was
back in a house from a distant period of my childhood.
Though the house itself was small, it was surrounded by
extensive grounds. In the middle of this great area, and
almost hidden by trees, there rose a huge warehouse full
of glass. I was playing, running through this huge yard
away from some imaginary enemy, when I fell onto the
glass. The cut in my leg was so deep that my flesh
instantly gaped open. It didn't hurt, in fact it seemed as
though I felt nothing except the interest of watching the
wound open and from the gash the blood flowing down
into the earth. I tried to close the wound with my hands,
but the bleeding didn't stop. I had no pain, but the
awareness of my open flesh, the spectre of slicing glass,
and the vastness of the land that had so frightened me.
Someone I didn't know came from the house to help
me, since I had started screaming when I saw myself
covered in blood.

Gradually my mind was taken over by another image.
I saw our bitch bleeding – bleeding and howling. No,
she wasn't howling, but making a similar, gentler sound
and all the while she was bleeding from below like a
sick woman. The bitch was already old, but old as she
was, she was dragging herself along on her belly leaving
a trail of blood behind her. She had started bleeding

days earlier when she went into labour, moaning like a woman in pain.

My grandmother said she wouldn't survive, that the bitch would die because she was too old to have puppies and that she'd signed her own death sentence. The last few days the sight of her painfully sliding and dragging her belly around was pitiful. She was a small dog, a mongrel who appeared one day and settled into a corner of the house to make a place of her own.

She had already had several litters but I had never been there then. It was my grandmother who had taken care of drowning the female pups and of finding homes in the neighbourhood for the males. I never witnessed this; I never saw her doing it and only know it happened because she told me.

But this time it happened differently. Day after day the whimpering and the bleeding continued – all the signs that forcibly reminded me of what was about to happen. I didn't dare touch her, I simply left her food even though it was clear that the bitch was by now quite incapable of eating. My grandmother kept saying how old the bitch was but this didn't help her and it didn't seem to me a sufficient reason to do nothing about the creature's agony.

The day came when the bitch could no longer walk. She began dragging herself along holding her hind legs stiff, leaving ever bigger and darker bloodstains on the floor. That day she also started the most desperate whining and my grandmother formally pronounced that the bitch was about to whelp. She said I'd have to help, that I'd have to deliver the puppies, that the bitch wouldn't make it on her own and that, if I didn't help, she would die with the pups still inside her.

Very gently I put the dog in her box. I leaned over beside her side and noticed that she was twisted and shaken by powerful contractions. I saw she was dying with a lump protruding between her paws. She was still bleeding and her hair was standing on end. I helped her. With my fingers I pulled at the first lump and one by one out came the puppies, looking like fat worms. I delivered five and then went to tell my grandmother. She told me to bring her the pups and a bowl of water. Although I understood what she wanted, I wasn't sure I could do it. But I did. I held each of the little animals up to the light and she nodded or shook her head accordingly. It was the three little female pups that I drowned, unable to stop crying as I held them under the water.

The poor bitch went on suffering for another two days. She was slowly dying. The two male pups also died. My grandmother was so ill that I didn't tell her, but I think she knew anyway. Despite being worn out, she instinctively knew everything that went on in the house. I cleaned up the blood. It was very difficult to get out the blood stains. Afterwards I remembered the man. Ah yes, that was the first time I had seen a man and I couldn't stop laughing at the old fellow with his trousers down. Perhaps he wasn't so old, but that is how I saw him – an old man with his trousers down, standing in the street expecting me to scream. No, I don't know, I can't imagine what he was expecting.

Yes, I do know. He wasn't expecting anything, nothing more than that I should notice that he was a man rather than any old thing, not an animal or a bit of rubbish, but a real man. And I did notice. I can't remember his face or his expression, I can't remember anything except his inescapably male part. In fact I took it in quite normal. It was like looking at the p one's hand, but knowing that from that day could deceive me. Although the heat at that tr was suffocating, it didn't bother me because so conscious of my good luck – without witnesses, without words, seduced by the force and distance of that image.

I think he moved off as I followed him with my gaze until he disappeared round a corner. That man's skin was a disaster. I remember his legs as a great mass of pus and dried blood from top to toe. From the waist down he seemed like a bird in agony.

Afterwards I vaguely remember some kind of a fall. It wasn't a fall, but something like a fall and with the effect of my banged head and drug-induced drowsiness I was amazed by the coldness of the woman and the incessant pecking of her instruments. I am still haunted to this day by the fractured memory of her ordering me to be silent, telling me not to try to close my legs because if I do the flow of blood will be more regular. She lifts up one hand and I see her white glove soaked in blood. It is impossible to describe my terror at the sight of the instrument she is holding. 'Keep still,' she says, insistently. In the end I lie still flat on my back with the woman standing staring at me. I think that I smiled. Yes, now I was smiling. 'Pull down your skirt,' she said. 'Go to sleep for a while.' It was then that the fist landed on my head and I was certain that my eyeball had burst. I have relived the moment of the blow, the moment I almost lost an eye. And although I would rather forget, for ever after I have imprinted on my mind the image of the narrow stretcher and her body half covered by a sheet. Dramatic evidence of her disease, her blood pressure was going down. I tried to cover her body with mine because it seemed to me that she was too visible right there in the hospital ward, but I couldn't manage to protect her. I witnessed the insertion of the needle into her vein. A trickle of blood ran down her right arm. Her arm already bore the traces of countless injections and the blood effectively hid these pitiful scars. When Sergio told me that Manuel had been detained in the South, I experienced a void, a hiatus. I thought of travelling to that area that I still did not know. I thought of death.

. . . .

Overwhelmed by compassion, I got into the habit of contacting Manuel by telepathy. With my head thus jammed, it refused to take in the countless changes that were taking place in the city. In a way I counted on Sergio, but he demonstrated extraordinary fortitude, though at times an ironic or even cruel expression showed through, but so subtle that there was no way of deciphering his true feelings. He was waiting for me wherever I went, looking at me in different ways so urgently that I began to be alarmed. At that stage I thought I should get rid of his burdensome presence, but he told me that if I did, death would be the only outcome of the war between them.

'I won't give you a break,' he said. 'I shan't let you have a moment's respite.'

I was both terrified and touched and got used to his constant devotion, to his questions, to his eagerness to know the slightest turn of my thoughts. He was ahead of me, always ahead, asking for details, demanding precise answers, alert to my endless contradictions, forcing me to the point of exhaustion to refine my huge mountain of lies.

He was my daily life, while secretly the imprint of Manuel remained between my sheets, on my blankets, under my pillow. Manuel occupied my mind. Those nights he appeared as a being far more solemn than he had ever been in real life. He appeared groaning, and his groans formed themselves into words I couldn't ever quite decipher; he appeared naked pursued by a flock of birds screeching 'blasted conformist' at him as he groaned, muttering those words that I could never manage to catch.

He was groaning in the depths of the night just as I would later, also naked and groaning, hounded by Sergio who finally and horribly humiliated me with a hatred matched only by my own. But Manuel was then far away in the night. He was still in detention in the South, together with all his family, his tongue tied while mine nimbly wove endless tales that Sergio committed to memory without forgetting even the most innocent incidents, to employ them later against me.

···········

Manuel lurked somewhere in the night. Detained down in the South he began to lose reality for me. I saw him as a ghost with many different faces. It was no longer Manuel. It was a chorus of hideous cackling voices that lay in wait for me in the night, demanding that I exact some kind of vengeance. Feverish, sweating, consumed with desire, I imagined my flesh criss-crossed with a tracery of knife wounds. The blood that I bled was the only response. The blood staining my legs. For nights on end I let the blood run down my legs, run for three harsh days and nights. To think of those nights, with blood gently flowing over my ankles, my insteps, the floor, my sheets soaked in my dreams.

Since I had no pain, the image of my blood became a huge flock of birds all flying at unimaginable speed. The blood had to flow to avert my own death sentence; I had to invent everything in those benighted hours, I had to uncover death constantly moving through the byways of my body. I was ending up soaked in my own blood so as not to forget what blood was. I was not dying but I was bleeding. Manuel was in detention in the South and with my blood I suspended his sentence for one more night.

It was now that I began to learn to do with very little sleep – with so little that all my muscles went into spasm. It was either my sleep or their death. I thought that if I were to stay asleep they would die in their hundreds. I felt as though I was falling apart, that the city might explode in all directions. With my mind I could just make out what was happening and happening. I didn't try to stop it because I needed to stay attached to violence in order to be level with the other violence. All I did was useless and exaggerated, but I carried on. And the blood kept coming, every month the blood came; and by then blood had lost all association for me but its irrevocable connection to death.

. . . .

Sergio was seeking in me an image that he'd held in his head since he was more or less a child. As we walked through the centre of the city – the city centre was one of the places where I most strongly felt under surveillance – he talked to me about the forgotten Francisca.

To her name he added a body with its own intense story. To begin with I thought Sergio was teasing, but when I saw his face I realised that the past had devoured all his energy. Taken aback by what he said, I tried to get out of the conversation but Sergio was completely caught up in the memory of his great passion and kept going back again and again to what she was like. What, precisely, was in that look? What did her smile mean? He kept repeating the same process of interrogation, trying to clarify the import of each gesture.

However intolerable I knew it to be, I realised that I was facing a man obsessed by a repetition that was out of control. When I realised he was forcing me into the same mould, I felt a sense of danger stretched taut between my temples.

five

....

francisca

He met Francisca at school. He noticed her as soon as she walked into the classroom. Sergio found going to that school really difficult. A strange place decreed by his mother, who was always dragging him off into one new situation after another. He felt uneasy and kept staring at Francisca. She looked at her watch, quite indifferent to her surroundings. Sergio realised that her watch must be new and was carried away by this fascinating observation. Sensing the intensity of his stare, Francisca lifted her head and in that brief second's exchange he knew that he had captivated her. Although he knew that his look was molesting her, he didn't let up. He answered the inquisitive questions of the other pupils without for a minute taking his eyes off her. He lost track of what he was saying, engrossed by the unease with which she struggled up from her bench to escape his insistent presence.

That was their first encounter. The next day he managed to find out everything about her, asking people casually as if it was not the least important. Meanwhile he carried on gazing at her, and went on gazing at her for weeks until she was quite used to his persecution.

Soon he began following her quite openly right to the door of her house; he started walking round the block, longing for it to be dark so he could start preparing for the following morning. Things that used to trouble him were relegated to a misty second place; her image – sitting on her school bench or smiling or walking through the city – completely blotted out all his earlier worries. It took him only three or four days of intensive surveillance to discover that Francisca, though only fourteen, already had a vice that he was happy to satisfy. He went on watching her for the whole of that year at school. Over the months he got used to keeping her in his mind, acting out scenes with her, combining them together at night, submitting her to the movements of his as yet undeveloped imagination.

He took nightly precautions to elude his mother who was on the watch out for symptoms. Every morning she brazenly examined his sheets – those sheets he shared with Francisca, stimulated by the distance between them and on fire with indifference.

He maintained a delicate refusal to speak to her; not a single sentence escaped him the whole year, as if afraid that speech could erode something important, that talking could break the fragile thread between them – and he was not prepared to surrender even the tiniest part of what he was feeling. He lived in a state of concentrated violence that had previously been dispersed among countless other phobias and hatreds; Francisca had managed to fuse it all, keeping him in a state of permanent insecurity, so watchful that the minutest detail became the focus of his life.

She knew very well what was happening and, with a degree of concentration equal to his own, stayed just as watchful, warning him that, though his obsession gave her some pleasure, there was a limit and she could offer nothing but passivity to their relationship. What she could not know was that he had chosen her precisely because of her character – this character that Francisca was trying her utmost to tame. For this reason Sergio never let so much as a single look betray how well he knew her and he devised a particular look just for her which made it seem as if he were looking at someone else – at that certain someone Francisca was hopelessly trying to catch.

It was a complete miracle that they kept their silence that whole year, without speaking out even once, despite sharing hours in the confined space of the school room, elaborating endless strategies to avoid talking to one another. After a year of observing her, of possessing her in every way he could imagine, he finally seemed to be moving towards the reality of speech. Francisca by now silently dictated his every move and imposed the necessary terms. Like an animal, guided by his sense of smell, he sniffed her out to get the measure of her, to fathom the power of her look, an omen of the exact moment when he would start to take advantage of the enormity of her growing vice.

As the end of the school year drew to a close, he wondered how he was going to get by without her. That first summer, the summer characterised by its absence of words, was the most suffocating he ever had to get through and to make it more bearable he pushed his body to its limits. Day and night he grappled with it, thus fending off pain and anxiety. Without paying attention to his mother or taking notice of anything that went on round him, he didn't even notice the creaking of his bed from which he never rose except when unavoidable.

···········

'Give me more drops. I prefer drops to injections.'

'No, you can't take any more. I've told you that you can't have any more.'

'But I can't stand them. I can't bear injections.'

'They're to make you sleep. You must sleep.'

'OK, but do it in the other arm, in my right one. Francisca, tell me – who is it who is walking around, just outside?'

'No one, there's no one there. Who on earth would want to come round at this time of night?'

· · · · · · · · · · ·

(There were other nights, still worse than this – but this was the night that made the strongest impression on me, perhaps because I touched her naked body and felt in her flesh her curtailed future. She was dying. She had started dying long ago. Oh God. I imagined the weight of the flock of birds falling on to her flesh. . .)

· · · · · · · · · · ·

After this immobile summer Sergio was scared of meeting Francisca. He had dreamed, imagined, suffered so much that he was afraid he had exhausted her and could come face to face only with his own alienation. He moved among the countless bodies, the feverish agitation on the faces of his fellow pupils on the first day of term. He couldn't see Francisca anywhere and withdrew into an inner state of crisis. He felt as though he was drowning, as though the walls were crushing him. He thought she must have moved to a different school, then realised that nothing had changed; that she was still alive inside him, as alive as his desire to look at her, to possess her, to attack her.

She appeared just as he was about to ask after her. Her presence filled him with such elation that he could not prevent himself from walking up to her and confronting her. Francisca became flustered and didn't lift her head until she sensed that something or someone had come between them. As though transported, he was unable to take his eyes off her, quite unable to smile, to speak or to move. He gazed at her and felt the summer's discomfort draining away. He could read his own story in Francisca's face; what was about to happen was the drift of this story. He saw her walk forward, he let her walk away and watched her until he lost her among the figures of the pupils in the noisy playground.

He remained transfixed in the middle of the corridor, revisualising her face, her expression. One thing hammered into his brain. Francisca looked different. There was something new about her face and in her way of walking. It was something so tenuous that his eye alone could catch it. He realised that Francisca had held a man between her thighs this summer and an uncontrollable rage almost knocked him back against the wall.

The morning passed without his noticing anything but the devastation of his own thoughts. At the end of school he waited for her at the gate and blocked her way. In alarm Francisca tried to sidestep him, but he seized her by the shoulders and demanded to know what had gone on that summer. She started to laugh, laughing as if he had just said the funniest thing she had heard in her life. In that moment Sergio experienced the full violence of being abandoned.

He spent hours that afternoon going round in circles, thinking over what had happened, remembering her laugh, feeling that he would never survive the shame.

That night's dream shocked him into a sudden relief
and into the recovery of some semblance of sanity. The
next morning he established that they faced a whole day
of classes together. Francisca as usual, withdrawn into
her customary indifference, scarcely looked at him.

Towards midday all that had gone before began to
seem quite unreal, but something deep inside him had
changed. He could not rid his head of the idea that
Francisca was different, though another part of him
persisted in clinging to the idea of gazing at her and the
pleasure of that gaze. By lunchtime the contradiction
was tearing him apart.

After school as usual he followed her out, into the last
heat of the season. His thoughts of the previous day
seemed absolutely right. Francisca's features had
changed, and in their alteration he saw with absolute
certainty the imprint of another man. He went on
searching for signs and though he knew that he could
not prove anything by looking, he went back to gazing
at her, assembling the clues and mulling them over.
Francisca has had a man this summer, he thought, and
the sentence went on echoing to the rhythm of his
loathing. The pressing need for revenge set itself like
steel in the nerve cells of his brain.

The heat fed into his impatience and upset his normal
equanimity. Francisca was only a few paces ahead of
him and it seemed to him that she was brazenly flaunting
her shamelessness. He looked at her now as at a woman
and it disturbed his nocturnal fantasies. He realised he
was heading towards a new reality and his suffering
changed in its very essence. He felt anguish and
delighted in that anguish she was causing him. He
looked fixedly at the figure walking ahead of him and

could distil the fear from Francisca's bones, tracing a
fine line of pain the length of her slender skeleton.

············

'Sort it all out, Francisca. Find the photos and the
papers. I want to leave all my things in order. No one
else must get involved. Let's make an inventory and
anything useless we'll chuck out.'

'I'm tired. I haven't the energy to go looking through
that junk in the cupboard. There's no rush. The things
are there and they'll still be there next week or next
month.'

'They are my things and I don't want them scattered
round just any old how. It won't take long to finish the
job I've given you. I'm sure that you can take a break
very soon.'

'Don't say that. It's the same every day. You are
simply calling for death, you've been calling it for years.
What you really want is to leave me on my own, to go
away leaving me alone and taking your papers with you.
You would even take my memories if you could.'

'What on earth are you talking about? Is this what I
brought you up for – so you could insult me when I'm
only one step away from my grave?'

'OK, tomorrow we'll sort things out, but I know very
well that you will simply sleep, leaving me to do all the
work on my own.'

············

(Her body completely lost its shape. It turned into
formless, dissipated flesh without bones, which I tended
throughout those long nights of her indescribable pain.
She had shed everything, even her rage. Once her anger

was gone, my terror began. I tried to provoke her, to graft her flesh back on to life, but she was beaten and had already succumbed to resignation without thinking of me. At the end I realised that she wasn't even thinking of herself . . . The flock of birds. I knew that the flock of birds was gathering anger that night.)

···········

Sergio was aware that his obsession caused astonishment in the classroom. By now everyone knew of his feelings for Francisca and he waited patiently, without changing his behaviour, for the gossip to die down. He simply smiled at the jokes, the hints and the running commentary without losing sight of Francisca who appeared completely self-absorbed, as if she were reaching the most complicated turning point of her life.

He realised that she was about to take the wrong turning and became terrified on his own account. He was obsessed by a girl who had lost the race before she'd even begun and he shuddered at the realisation that it was precisely this that attracted him – the hope of seeing her teetering on the edge of the abyss and of witnessing her final fall. Francisca was his salvation. This attachment to her destruction was Sergio's only hope of avoiding his own loss of equilibrium. But he was afraid he had foreseen something which would finally crush him under its great weight.

All this time, he felt crushed by his discovery, as though shackled and asphyxiated. Francisca's pallor made his sickly pining harder still to bear and for the first time he sought to be apart from her. He wanted to test his own vitality with someone else and longed feverishly for health.

He decided to stop following her. The day he broke
his habit and went out without Francisca, he noticed his
strength return in an over-violent surge of energy. He
paced the streets, able at last to differentiate buildings,
the shapes of trees, the exact temperature of the air.
When he got home he lay down and listened to music.
As he fell asleep he drifted back into his habit of
dreaming of Francisca, but now his imagination evoked
her as a figure eroded by time. A sense of the past
flooded him with nostalgia. Other girls came into his
head and he decided to choose one. He wanted to finish
with Francisca once and for all and in his mind he had
worked out the perfect way of doing it. He took her
standing upright in the whiteness of infinity, in a mighty
sexual battle.

A knock on his door quickly brought him back to his
senses. When he opened it, there was Francisca. He
couldn't say anything because she, stubborn and rigid,
reminded him that it was he who had started the ritual
of following her through the city, and now the city was
still threatening her. At that, Sergio realised he had been
fooling himself and went back to performing the inexorable ceremony.

They hammered out the details of their truce and he
sat back down on the sofa. There on the narrow sofa he
succeeded in completely unbuttoning her blouse and
struggled to take it off with his left hand while his right
hand moved up her clenched legs which nevertheless
opened enough to let him progress a little way up.

It bothered him that Francisca never closed her eyes,
as if she were a spectator at her own performance. At
first this habit of hers paralysed him, but he overcame
that by keeping his own eyes shut. He realised he had

only a few minutes but she made no movement so, despite knowing that it might wreck everything, he took her hand and placed it on his trousers. At this, Francisca got up from the sofa and looked down at him defiantly, but without doing up her blouse.

Sergio pushed her against the wall and she tried to escape from his grasp, but his hand had already undone his trousers and, for once, he was not even remotely afraid of seeming ridiculous. He watched Francisca and saw in her eyes an expression of a remote hatred, a hatred of which his own was but a pale reflection. It dawned on him that he should leave, but his inflamed body shut off his reason and he only came to his senses when he heard Francisca telling him to stop.

He felt desperately cheated. He looked at her again and saw on her face the unmistakable shadow of his own ridiculousness and it filled him with an uncontrolled violence.

· · · · · · · · · · ·

'It would be better to bring your bed into the room. It's so cold you'll freeze to death with having to get up so much in the night.'

'I'd already decided to do that. I'll get it changed tomorrow.'

'Francisca, have you thought what you'll do when I'm finished?'

'No, I never think about that. Please, don't talk about such things.'

· · · · · · · · · · ·

(It was a total disintegration, with her body exploding out through every pore. There wasn't a single tiny area of her skin untouched by the disease as it slowly, terribly, hatefully advanced. An illness seemingly with no end; in fact with neither beginning nor end . . . A flock of birds, I imagined the flock flying off with the carrion trapped in their beaks.)

. . . .

Sergio felt troubled, uncomfortable, ill at ease. After everything that had happened in Francisca's house, he had decided to rid himself of the whole ridiculous affair. But now she followed him, seeking him out with great determination. He knew that she had trapped him crazily with the intense feeling she'd spread in the furthermost extremities of his body. Then she'd leave him on some street corner – always a different one – to make his own way home in the threatening dark.

At a party she egged him on to lock themselves in a room, running the risk of discovery by the other guests who were simply waiting for a scandal to erupt. He forgot the danger of lying with Francisca who, unbiddable, would withdraw before he could consummate what their hiding place had led him to expect. Beside himself with rage, he had to find relief in the bathroom to rid himself of his desperate wanting. His tenuous peace of mind was already shaken by the earlier times when they used to play, cuddling on the narrow sofa. Then he had thought he could give Francisca up, but he reached such a pitch of anxiety that he had to admit that he never stopped waiting for her, that he was always longing for her – on street corners, in small rooms, on beaten-up sofas. The desire to lie with her gave him a permanent ache in his groin.

Soon he got used to any peculiarity. He even got used

to sharing her. He had an illness that kept him indoors for a fortnight and when he recovered he walked up and down for hours, waiting for her man to leave the house, without minding the rain – which in fact helped to soothe his overheated brain.

Sergio had learned to wait. He had acquired the habit as a child and with Francisca he was practising it to perfection. She had finished with boys and had now moved on to men. He could only imagine that the man, spending so long inside the house, was being given a thorough lesson in getting to know a girl.

He knew perfectly well that Francisca did her utmost to escape anything that would tie her down, even though her nomadic soul would always seek out someone to hold her steady. When the man finally left, Sergio just glimpsed her standing in the doorway. They exchanged an ironic glance which left them unperturbed. He supposed there would be no end to this. Neither time nor circumstance could assuage the sharpness of his passage. But then came the accident and, having broken his plaster cast, he broke with Francisca too. The excruciating pain of the double fracture to his arm cleared his brain. As he smashed his arm against a tree and the plaster cast flew into fragments, pain brought him back to his senses.

He realised that it was cracking – that unbearable feeling which kept him endlessly on the move, seeking out Francisca in her every coming and going, always slipping out of his reach. The harshness of it was made up for by the calm with which they could now hold conversations, though there was still desperation beneath the surface of their words and in his eager desire for survival he was in fact plunging headlong.

With Francisca, anything was possible but it was also uncertain. She tried out various systems disguised by indifference, but he very soon realised that he needed these tricks. Terrified, he told her so. His fear hovered in an uncharted twilit zone of cheap hotels, dingy streets, and other people's beds.

There were no limits and it was shattering; and it was Francisca who was encouraging him, forcing him to take part in new scenes. He no longer knew how to possess her without the promise of seeing her possessed by other men, without the promise that he would possess other women so that she in turn could watch him. In such acts Francisca sharpened his hunger to the point of hatred. Once apart he could do no more than bear the weight of his sordid existence.

Before Sergio broke his arm, Francisca had been persistently provocative. She humiliated him, then retreated without allowing him to follow her. It was in one of these moments of confusion that he broke his arm. Making some unaccountable move, he fell, and the impact was the cause of the fracture. Partially immobilised by his plaster cast, he could scarcely manage the complicated movements she demanded of him.

In their last hotel room, Sergio finally responded in the ultimate and only way left to him. No longer master of himself, he punched her with his good arm. He punched her in the eye with his clenched fist, and only then did she cling to him to make love more perfectly than they had ever done before. That very night Sergio began his escape.

The following day he met Francisca looking so calm that he began to think he had made a mistake. But she openly begged him for more. She was speaking as they were walking past a tree and, without understanding what dark force drove him, Sergio smashed his broken arm against the trunk. This double fracture, this redoubled pain finally ruptured the poisonous cord that had bound him to Francisca.

············

'Don't ring anybody. It was the meal, what you gave me to eat, that made me ill.'

'But suppose no one comes today. It's very late already and you must sleep.'

'I'm fine. I've already told you it was something I ate.'

'OK, you certainly seem all right. You look much better these last days.'

············

(The truth is that it was the only thing left. I was always looking, searching everywhere for something to hang on to, but there was nobody. She told me stories, but I discovered one day they were all lies. There was nobody. 'It's true, isn't it – there is no one there but you?' I asked her. Just as I thought she was going to respond, she turned away. At night, when she was organising her papers, she said, 'I don't know what's going to happen to you when I'm not here. What will you do?' For a few moments the world turned upside down. I imagined the flock of birds so vast they darkened the evening sky.)

six

....

habit

Manuel was suffering in the South. I began to realise
that his suffering became more acute in step with the
increased danger at night. Without concrete evidence I
could only protect myself with my motionless vigil,
hoping to diminish the level of his pain. It was no longer
Manuel, scarcely even his body, that was now being
subjected to ever greater demands. My terror blossomed
at night, each and every night, clamouring for the right
for him to breathe. 'Don't stop breathing', I remember,
was my most regular prayer. 'Don't stop breathing', in
an awareness that the whole of life depended on a
breath. It was no longer Manuel, it was scarcely even a
body playing games, confusing itself with my body,
sapping my dwindling vitality. They were suffering and
blaming me in the secrecy of those intense nights.

'Don't stop breathing', and Manuel looked at me with
scorn as if to say 'Fucking bitch', while I tossed and
turned between my sheets, driven mad by the absence
of pleasure. Every single part of my body was racked
with longing for those other bodies to be restored so that
I could breathe again. At night I was almost suffocating,
confused, pleading on their behalf for everlasting life.
They laughed at me, they tormented me. Manuel took
his revenge by not making the slightest effort to over-

come his own suffering. Perhaps he actually wanted to die and fought against his own breathing in the cold depths of night. I was sleeping very little by now, very little indeed. The image of Manuel allowed me no rest.

Manuel had been detained in the South along with his whole family. My muscles no longer worked properly and my breathing had become very faint from lack of sleep. My breath began to come very slowly, it cost such an effort to breathe through the night. Terrified by the threat to my own survival, I tried to put an end to these sensations by planning a journey to the South. I felt I had to go to the South to discover exactly what was happening to Manuel. I couldn't tell that I was about to undertake a doomed journey and that Pucatrihue was all that was left of the South.

. . . .

Poverty now began to catch us in a vicious circle. Ana occasionally helped me out with a little money. Ana liked everything I did and we disliked the same things too. I was almost going under with shortages of everything; when things got unbearable I would run to her, until I reached the point where I regularly began to depend on her help even for my food. It was crushing, and I could see no way of changing my circumstances. Even the small job opportunities that used to bring in a little money seemed to have vanished from the horizon.

Poverty acquired a new value, holding us together, intensifying our desire, and carrying our aggression to its very limits. But Ana always seemed to have means and shared what she had with me. But in truth by now I began to feel increasingly hostile towards her because of her indirect way of making me pay. She wanted to take over my world, she tried to take everything I touched. She demanded that I share with her even the most complicated or most evanescent of my feelings, and the worst thing was her fixation on my memories of Manuel. She was fascinated by my fascination and wormed her way into my obsession, trying to steal my personal history. In her desire to get even closer, she ran to Sergio and treacherously broke a whole string of confidences – telling him stories of my life that only she knew. By betraying me she won his confidence and manoeuvred herself into a central position between us. At that stage I had to give in. Ana had been a friend since early childhood and I knew only too well how greedy she was. Betrayal was her way of doing things; affection was her way out. Sergio's permanent presence wavering between the two of us reawoke our earlier differences and made our meetings more abrasive.

What Sergio never grasped was that the bond between Ana and myself was unbreakable and her betrayal was only a temporary hitch. Ana had latched on to my construct, the world I had stubbornly insisted on building since meeting Manuel, so she could carry on the erratic argument started when she took the first boy I'd seduced.

When I arrived at that party I already knew what I was going to find. Although I was slow in drawing the obvious conclusion, I'd finally succeeded in piecing it all together. I decided to recover my integrity and went, though I knew I'd be put in an intolerable position.

For the first time I drank *pisco* and the strength of the spirits burned my throat. At that party too, so long ago now, I smoked my first cheap cigarette, deliriously happy. The boy arrived as we'd agreed and his face seemed even more radiant than I'd remembered. If I hadn't finally put two and two together, I would have carried on in ignorance with Ana humiliating me behind my back.

I remembered everything I had ever told her, each of the boy's advances and what it felt like when he ran his hands over me. I also remembered Ana's expression and her eagerness to hear every detail, every fragment, every word. I remembered her advice to take things further, to go the whole way. When the boy came over we danced very close, but then I acted on a sudden strong impulse. I left the boy in the middle of the dance floor and walked over to Ana. Took her and danced with her, telling her I loved her, telling her – the *pisco* speaking – that I hated her; and when I finally decided I was fed up with drinking and smoking, I aimed a blow that Ana either couldn't or chose not to duck.

···········

Ever since that first party we started treating each other in an oblique way that paradoxically succeeded in keeping us close for quite a time. Ana was my cousin and perhaps being family made us better able to weather the feuds, the threats, the arguments. But I was not going to let Manuel have her. She wanted to snatch my pleasure away in order to deprive me of affection. It had happened before. More than once I had colluded in such scenes, but that was at the time when my grandmother was dying, her whole body ravaged by disease, and I was the only witness of the horrific mutilation.

···········

Ana knew Manuel well. I've already said that Ana knew everything I knew. The first time they were together I knew instantly that she was waiting for something. Manuel was laughing, drinking and laughing and drinking, till I realised he was on the point of touching her. Manuel could not resist provocation. Ana was incapable of not being provocative.

I chose to stay on the sidelines and to let them explore the shape of each other's bodies. My only attempt at self-preservation was to step back from my emotions so I could watch them from a neutral position and analyse the detail of their coming together. Consumed by desire, awkward, revoltingly eager, they stumbled about in front of me, colliding with the banalities of their own manoeuvres. I remained safely clear-headed, but could see that they were trying to make me lose all confidence. They never managed to slake their desire because they were quite devoid of intensity. At that stage Ana and Manuel were incompatible and I was the only connection that they could refer to. Their first disagreements arose as the night wore on and Manuel held his position by fencing with words. Ana was less good at that game and could not fend off the attack. She turned pale and recoiled to concentrate on avoiding the confrontation. I felt myself bursting with anger, watching the delicacy with which the two of them built up and demolished their mutual images. They were playing games the whole time and I couldn't help feeling resentful. Everything round me was pretty vague by this stage, so vague that there was room for them to confuse me thoroughly. To be honest, I didn't know what was going on. Perhaps Ana and Manuel did nothing at all, perhaps they were only exchanging commonplaces.

After three months without, I had begun bleeding again and entered a phase of extreme vagueness. I was solely concerned with the flow of my own blood and felt full of an impossible desire. I wanted to be curled up in a ball under my own skirts and to crawl up between my legs. I wanted to be the towel that held the flow and contained the blood clots. How I would have loved to move up till I was inserted between my legs, moving up and up until I had penetrated the source of my blood. When Ana and Manuel got to know one another, a faint dislike set in. I couldn't achieve the slightest rapprochement between them. That day I started bleeding again after a break of three months and I felt very out of sorts.

············

Ana spent one perfect night with Manuel. She told me about it quite unexpectedly, knowing in advance how hopelessly caught up I would become in her reminiscences. She went into a detailed description of her expensive, provocative outfit, and I could visualise her walking forward, her legs deliberately restricted by her shiny black dress. Ana confessed that she was so driven by her depraved desire that night that she consciously sought to focus people's looks on the violent rippling of her thighs, barely disguised beneath the shiny black material. I watched her smiling and it hurt.

I saw her coming into the dance hall with Manuel, that same hall from which I had fled as from the plague when I had first recognised the murderous intensity of my own feeling. Ana came into the hall flaunting her body and told me how the spotlights flattered her hair which she had slicked with some oil to enhance its bold natural brilliance. She said she knew it worked because she had tried it out exhaustively. She picked up her glass with her highly painted fingernails and with that one classic gesture set in train the obscene future of Manuel's desire. As the glass reached her lips, Manuel understood that she had become a totally sexual being.

But what a tragedy – I saw her dazzle that perverse dance hall, with the gleam of triumph hidden between her legs. I watched her renounce speech, in favour of the power of an insufferable brazenness. I can still see Manuel coming into that dance hall to finish his seduction. I watched them smile and bury their sexual differences in the instant it took them to go on to the dance floor. There, in age-old fashion, they resolved the crisis that held them balanced on the brink of an imaginable act.

Ana exploded into dance. She was absolutely brilliant. That dance completely robbed me of my own savagery. Shielded by conniving bodies, Manuel masturbated in the darkness while Ana knowingly moved her right hand faster and faster with a rhythmical and ancient movement. To the beat of the music, I could imagine Manuel's outline reeling every which way, and in his depraved ecstasy staining the shiny black material of Ana's dress – his revenge.

Manuel still had not had enough. How wouldn't I know what it took to satisfy him? Ana urged him to go out into the city to revisit the old quarter where the two of them were shielded from the brilliance of the night. Like animals on heat, they went in and out of places where naked bodies moved gracefully, ceaselessly, with no let up. I could easily understand their passage, for I too had loitered perniciously.

I foresaw the meeting of their two naked bodies. On

the verge of tears I had to listen to every last syllable of Manuel's words, struggling as he moaned. Are you moaning? Yes, you are. I know that moaning, it has always been there, between my legs, my most precious belonging.

She told me that they went to sleep quite drained. In the morning daylight distanced them. Such violence. Manuel wanted to masturbate. Don't say it, don't say anything – he was masturbating to annihilate her, begging her to watch him, just to watch him, so he could show up the difference that separated them. That dawn, driven by the mockery of daylight, he couldn't stem the dreadful intensity of the previous night's sensations.

It was an appropriation, an assault on *my* black dress, *my* hairspray, the nightmare of my own behaviour on the dance floor where, overcoming my better judgement and my prejudice, I sought Manuel's hand so he should touch me, touch me below in my pleasure, taking no notice of the other bodies, nor of my sudden unexpected moaning in the middle of the dance floor, in the dangerous proposition of the dance; moaning, moaning because it was escaping, my life was seeping away with each heartbeat. The entreaty issued with my blood. All that night I bled and in my base desperation, scarlet, wet, cried out my need for his caresses there in that slender strip of flesh through which my life had so often ebbed.

I gave up his mouth, his tongue, his saliva, for his hand, since there in that public place, overwhelmed by this need, there was not a single corner where I could lie down and beg him to staunch the flow with his tongue. For this he returned at night, croaking in the night, when all that remained was the darkness. Manuel

was still in detention in the South and Ana said anything
that occurred to her in her attempt to destroy me.

············

Out of the blue my body began to betray me. My flesh
spilled over, exposing me to people's looks and the
danger of those looks. I had to avoid being noticed in
the city, I had to erase the slightest indication of lust.
Deprived, chronically anorexic, I began to feel permanently sick. Manuel was in detention in the South and I
could no longer visualise his shape. His body had
dissolved, my memory of his features was utterly frag-
mented. Except at night. Night was the right time for
flesh and surrender to tactile domination.

Hunger pursued me and distanced me yet further
from the tangible world. My body was in a state of
permanent demand and the faint echoes of Manuel that
I encountered seemed equally demanding. Without
knowing what it was he wanted of me I tried out
different responses to make him abandon me. Mentally
I veered towards disgusting things to eat. I found I was
beginning to fantasise about worms, left-overs, rotten
food, until I picked up a piece of decomposing meat and
ate my way slowly through it. I could manage the taste
but it failed to cure me of my craving. Afterwards an
attack of vomiting left me helpless for a few hours. I
desperately wanted to rid myself of the burden of this
unfair penance and asked Sergio for help to make it
through the night. I was worn out, beaten, and begged
him to keep me company in my struggle against the
destiny of my nights.

seven

....

the ten nights of francisca lombardo

Night falls, the moon is full, and I can see your distress by its light. We have made our plans, we have made so many plans that I am mollified. You ask me to talk and I can no longer hold my tongue. I climb on to you, warmed by my memories, moved by my own words. The bed is shaking and I no longer care about my freezing feet. Such brilliant red. I shall hold on to you for ever and you mount me, inflamed by my stories. Don't you have anything to tell me? – but lost in your intense concentration on your own rhythmic movements, you can't even hear me. Boom – you leap away like a wounded soldier, leaving me drowning. You move so I can't see you, and from the far side of the bed you redouble your promises, refine our plans. I don't believe a word of it – a deaf and blind bird moves only to the rhythms of its desires. That flattering, lying bird. You are holding the bird in your hand, its wings in my bed, and pretend you are sharing my dreams. Carefully I dry myself on the sheet and the bird flies over to me. How was it the first time? Francisca resists. Thursdays are funny days – laughter from morning to night. It was on a Thursday that they suddenly cut the minimum wage, when they smashed the workers. I made it with a day-labourer ruined after precisely three months. Francisca resists, anchored to the head of the bed with all my strength, thinking of the masterly articulation of the knee. He was not what one would normally call a day-labourer, or any kind of a worker, so lacking in expertise that there was no way of explaining things to him, one wouldn't know how. At that stage we hardly knew one another. I couldn't resist it, but it was beyond my understanding to see I was dealing with a battleground, a cavalcade, an invasion of undefended territory. The day-labourer's son made it with me. He twisted my right arm till I got cramp. I didn't tell you the truth about this, I didn't tell you anything that really happened. It is our lies that bind us, five years now of telling lies, and recently I've noticed that things no longer seem the same to me. No more my useless, expressionless bird. I don't want the dress you promised me, I want a different one. I want you to stay with me for ever; you tell me you will and I don't believe you. The first time, I lit up like a city of cement and metal, blazing with a thousand sparks from car headlights. My city self resisted, my urbane self. Now I hold on to you like an ancient avenue, like a badly tuned television. Images collapse, disintegrating in the vortex. Spread your wings and cover me. My feet are freezing, I touch you and you shiver. I am trying to snare each hair on your body, I am trying to pluck your wings. I still have so much to tell you – there were flocks of birds flying towards the city suburbs. Don't go to sleep, I'm talking to you. Listen carefully and don't think of anyone else. You are thinking of somebody else, of other things, you wretched, heartless bird, you old owl of ill omen. I am telling you lies to make up to you, and succeed so well that you hug me and I let you carry me off to the slippery place where we've been for the last five years, besieged by the man who has been following me to kill me and who at this very moment will be waiting with a splinter of glass to gouge out my eye. But now we are embracing and in desperation I believe everything you tell me, forgetting how this morning early I caught your look of loathing, that look of yours I know so well, that darts your eyes when your assassin bird is asleep. I laughed at you that night and you raised your hand to hit me in the face with heartrendingly human force.

. . . .

The bed creaks and creaks. It creaked and creaked in that miserable little room with its wobbly floorboards and peeling wallpaper. Me naked. He undressed me and I failed to respond. My naked body achieved a surprising independence – earning its own living, rearing up. The hidden animal in me woke from its den and risked almost anything. I risked everything and when he said 'Francisca,' I didn't even believe him. It wasn't me. It was the creature, not myself. It was my hand going up and down, my index finger. My heart's finger scratching a desperate declaration of love with its fingernail. I could not keep still. I felt as though a fighter bomber had gone crazy between my open legs. I felt as though I was about to be blinded in my right eye by a great spike which at the last moment swerved and thrust up between my legs. I felt as though my heart's fingernail was tunnelling through a cement wall. A sawmill, the blade of a propeller. With complete assurance he was preparing to go to work with his tongue. The bed wouldn't stop creaking, echoing to the noise of a woman outraged by what was happening. My brutalised body had lost all vision of terror. He ran his tongue along the soles of my feet. There was a twenty-five watt bulb in the room, and the benign gloom shone with saliva. The bed was held together with twisted wire: that damned creaking. His tongue embarked on one of my ears, stopping it with saliva to block out the noise. There was only one window in the room, a filthy skylight. It must have been about three in the afternoon, but you couldn't see daylight in this place. One of my nipples suddenly stood out, erect, then both nipples. His saliva soothed me, helped me to bear the birds' beaks. We didn't even have a lamp on the bedside table and I could scarcely make out my black shoe dropped in the middle of the room. I stopped looking. He put his tongue in my mouth and ran it over my teeth. I wanted his tongue, I desperately wanted his tongue, I longed to swallow his tongue. But none of this was me, it was the animal in me with its huge pink tongue, baying to get out. I was harshly honed to his tongue, gently honed to the room. My two nipples pressed his two eyes closed. He said he didn't want anything to do with me if I was bleeding, that he couldn't bear the sight of stained sheets.

'Are you bleeding?' he asked me.

'No,' I answered.

············

I follow you at night, at daybreak. All on my own I call you by name. What did you do to me? My legs and stomach are swollen. I have become so vulgar, so shockingly vulgar. How can I live with eyes so swollen I'm unable to tell the difference between a boy and a man? I can't even understand beauty any more – pretty

boys slip through my fingers. Where have the men gone?
I'm an expert. I'm wary of pretty girls – they want to
seduce me, to nibble me, to eat me up. But no longer. I
am so coarse that I now have the eyes of a cat. My
swollen eyes can even see what lies beneath the bed.
They are phosphorescent. I know that our bones are
depraved, hideously depraved. Oh, the animal in me.
The boy found it repulsive. When I said, 'Little bird,'
he took fright, he shrivelled up, he almost disappeared
altogether. He didn't know it, but he was coarse too –
he didn't know how to put names to things, he was so
afraid of words that he shrivelled up. Flushed. Let the
night come, let it be dark so he can open his legs and
piss on the floor of my room. Let night come. Cockroaches become invisible when wet with urine. There
was a cockroach in the lavatory with its legs flailing in
the air and I killed it – I killed a whole family of
cockroaches. My greedy animal self wants to graze, to
go out to pasture to browse and lie down, its four legs
under it. Spoil it. It's inhumane to keep it permanently
shut up. What animal? It was me. It was I who started
the quarrel with the boy. The only noise was my
shoulder grating against my bone. But a bird always
pecks. What a fate! There was one unimaginably crude
night. Francisca is running. I hadn't bathed for a week,
and by the end of the week my body was stinking.
Someone is following me. Soon I shall be twenty-two
and I'll look for work. I shall be just one more employee.
I'll work for a while and then I'll get sick and someone
will have to look after me. There is so little money it's
not worth fleeing into the night. The boy had no passion
for words, he was so scared his tongue only choked him
– that lying, shrivelled tongue. I shall leave my animal

to die upside down till it suffocates. I haven't got an animal. The bird pecks on monotonously – boom, boom. What an amazing ability, boom, boom. What can make it so decisive? My propaganda blazes and the bird pecks away at my own propaganda. It is dumb, quite dumb. The boy's body fled to lose itself in the night, that night when I attacked my own lower lip with my teeth. It felt like an animal, my upside down mouth, and I sensed the imminence of death. Death was waiting just outside my head for me finally to fall down, so it could catch me between its legs. Hide me for just one night. Any day now I'll be simply one more employee and anyone can sack me. I am still standing on my own two feet and refuse to be an animal sprawled on the mattress, refuse to wash like a cockroach wet with urine. Someone is following me. It's a noisy woman on all fours – how she shouts. In the next-door room a woman screamed and I couldn't help feeling enslaved by her scream. No longer. Any minute now I shall be twenty-two and I shall start on a new life as an employee, as yet one more employee, and my wages will enable me coldly to kill my animal. Through my swollen eyes I saw a clay dish, a little lamp and a strikingly beautiful green carpet on the floor. I stopped in front of the mirror and from there began my secret descent.

············

Did we talk that night? It's dark. Do you realise how dark it is? You got upset and I can't understand what I have done this time. I notice it in the dark. I spill a drop, scarcely even a drop, but you can't take even that one drop. You can't take anything, you tell me, but what you don't tell me is that I scare you with my bruised eye. Soon we'll know, we'll see who will win this battle, who will rout the night's loathing. You don't love me tonight, you don't love anyone, my self-absorbed bird. You are afraid of my weight and the weight of my grief. You are marked by terror, taken over by evil thoughts, which is why you come each night to my bed. I hear you enter like wonderful soft mountain music beautifully played on instruments whose strength you understand. You insulted me with your coming and going, in and out, but I saw your shadow. It's years ago now since I saw a shadow in my room and realised that I would lose an eye, that sooner or later it would be mercilessly gouged out with that spike and I would lose it. Won't you do anything? Won't you say anything? Not tonight. Tonight I should not take your weight so I want to mount you, to be on top. I climb a deafeningly dangerous man, a bird throttled in its tree. This time it felt as though I was being decapitated, I lost my head, I suffered, I paid the price from below. Is it you underneath now? Didn't I tell you? I'll talk to you and don't interrupt me, don't interrupt just as I'm on the verge of coming. If you stop now it will make me ill. My amazing hand is clever at keeping pace with my tongue, gently, slowly. The voluble world between my hand and my tongue is calming down. My tongue is growing larger through my hand. Everything is inside me. How I have changed. He called me; 'Francisca,' he said and I realised that he was off looking for a woman and felt myself surrender to the same depraved need. That compulsive night, my frenzied hand, my brain stripped bare. I was incapable of thought, so all my energy seeped down into my body. I'll bear one more night with you on top and it seems like a night of lies, as false as the stain spreading round my waist, like the scar at the edge of my pelvis, like the mole at the corner of my lip; only the erection of my nipples assures me that this is a real night I am facing. Take me out of myself, carry me away, tell me again what we will do together. I spent an extraordinary night of hostility, amid a flock of demented birds.

············

I need you. Tonight he is coming beneath me, and I am here, arched above him, my legs spread, waiting. My beautiful wound for ever between my legs. You sniff, you scratch, you augment the nightfall. The night won't open, won't open. Erect, erect, erect. You are flying up into the night my conceited bird and you talk to me. Go on, tell me, talk of your conquests. Did you like it very much? No? What was it you liked so much? You spin your words out carefully, while I try an impossible position, laying myself open to appalling risks. I am in this terrible position confronting the night, on the point of dissolution. Does blood have to matter to you? What really happens to you when you see blood? Tonight you are just another and I let you in like just another, as you know, with my legs spread. If you hadn't landed an attack on my mind, I could now reach the stronghold of your flesh. Erect, erect, erect. The intensity of my hand can achieve more than all your lies. If I use both my hands perhaps I can stave off the crisis of the night. My fingers hurt, my fingers in that mouth, the empty beauty of my wound. The noise is getting closer again. What are you going to give me? With what will you pay me for this? Look at my head. Never, not in a million years could they persuade me; it is priceless, it is not anything to do with being employed, it's not something a worker could do. But even knowing this, thinking about it, it didn't seem possible, but it has just happened. I have come on a lot, haven't I? I have taken a great step forward, and the other women are so furious that I need a painkiller to be able to bear them. You refuse to come up with the money, you don't want to pay me for my pains. You throw my addiction to tranquillisers in my face. I have no desire to listen to another word tonight and I think how common everything that you have done is, but I tell you yes, yes anything, to flatter you. You are so common it is almost embarrassing. I am embarrassed by my own self. What a spectacle I am making of myself. I'll do it well. Earlier I might have staggered around, not understanding what was wanted of me. I saw two bodies curled into one another and I was dazzled by their flexed muscles. You like mirrors, don't you? You don't like losing sight of yourself even for a second. I swear that this time I shall growl like an animal so you won't part from me and leave me facing the man who follows me to kill me and destroy my sight. It is tragic. I've guessed where the birds' hideout is. They have taken me on as a worker and I have to battle for my livelihood, arguing over each clause of my contract. And as for you, what are you doing? The man is outside walking meticulously from side to side, a bird eager to launch itself at me. It is bound to blind me. Stay with me tonight, don't allow me to humiliate myself by putting myself in this position. Every night. There is something slippery in me that stops me from taking the workers' side. I sense I shall lose my battle since the birds have retreated into blackest night and I can't make them out in the gloom.

I am only an employee, one worker among countless others, my body arched, my legs spread. You appear naked, shamelessly winged, with a delicate fringe of feathery down. Pausing above the bed you start arching over me, arching. You arch over me and gently start healing my terrible hurt.

....

You promise me that we'll stay together always and make me long to run away until I'm lost. I don't even know why you are staying. I've turned thirty, and you didn't give me a present or wish me a happy birthday. I am losing track of how old I am by your side. I wanted to be with someone else. I wanted it so badly, so desperately wanted a different body beside mine that day. The night of my thirtieth birthday you picked a fight with me while I was thinking of all those other people. What will become of them? Juan got a bicycle spoke embedded in his eye. I was there. Juan's cousin and I often used to shut ourselves in the bathroom and go swiftly, cursorily from head to toe. I took off my clothes and we walked across the cold tiles to lean against the lavatory. Outside the door I could hear footsteps – it was Juan with his eyeball hanging out. We had the water running, we let it run for an hour. That was fine. Juan lost an eye playing with his bicycle. I screamed that the eye was stuck on the spoke and his empty socket full of blood. Afterwards the two of us shut ourselves in with his cousin, while the water ran on, playing, the ambulance siren wailing, all of us. In there, we relaxed. Then from one day to the next I left the lot of them, and I didn't give them a thought on my thirtieth birthday. I put on a light-coloured suit for the celebration and I told you that I didn't want to fight, but the fight started when I told you what it was I had been longing for that day. At night the sheet was rumpled and you complained. You rumpled my pale suit but it was you who finished up in tears. I was terrified and my deviant age wandered in an absurd pilgrimage round the room, scared by my cries. You did nothing that could remotely be called having a celebration. You finished up crying because you couldn't take my years and absorb them yourself. The bird flew up to pin me to the bed. You pinned me to the bed to comfort me below as a present. You comforted my thirty years and the bird rose up, ineffably proud. You have come to tell me that we will stay together for always just as I am thinking of someone else, someone other than you. He is a handsome man who kissed me in the toilet and parted my legs with his knee. In front of the mirror. I saw my face in the mirror and realised that it was reversed. It wasn't my face that I saw, but the other side of my face and my right leg being thrust aside. I couldn't think about you. You told me that you would forgive me if only I would tell you everything, but it didn't happen like that, I didn't tell you everything, I didn't want to see the bird aroused, your obedient bird. Tonight I'm waiting for you with the sheets neatly smoothed and you roll over like a child who wants to play with me. Look out, I am more than thirty years old and I shan't let you. My animal commands me to calm down. I am calm. There's a man waiting for me outside in the street to put out my eye. In his hands he is hiding a nail to put out my right eye.

············

I can't find a job. They pay so little and no one believes me, not even you, you moaning bird who keeps throwing back in my face the fact that you support me. You stingy bird. I am not going to agree to work for a starvation wage just so that later you can carry on begging me to do things to you at night for free. I've already done more than enough for you for free and you don't even know how to say thank you, you don't appreciate anything. Let's not quarrel now, you tell me that you don't want any more arguments. I don't believe you, I don't believe you because you are keeping notes about me in a way I can't stand – I shan't let you, you'll never again win my consent. We will either do things my way or we won't do anything. There's nothing you want to do with me and you blame me for it, you pretend that it's my fault; but that's not so. I have sought you out in all kinds of ways and you won't rise, you are quite crestfallen – what's wrong with you? Look out, you might stay like that for ever, a dead and buried bird. Don't suffer, leave me to myself, leave me to proceed a little by little at a time and don't spring surprises on me. I know what you want of me tonight, but it's impossible. Do you want me to tell you something? Perhaps it will wake you up again and you'll respond. I am feeling better; actually to tell the truth I feel rotten, worse and worse, and I can't remember what you've talked to me about all this past year. I know you told me that my head has no future. The last time you made me jump out of bed, you shot me away, far away, you calligraphic bird. Now you tell me that you are frightened of me. Flutter round, don't be afraid, and massage the bruises on my stomach. Don't look at me, stop looking at me since I don't know what to do, I don't know how to be, seeing that you don't like the way I was before. You want me to tell you about the episode in the park and I can't remember what I told you before. I don't want to get it wrong because if I do you will lose your feathers and collapse. I am seriously worried for you. Do you wish you were with another woman? If you dare, my cheating bird, what you say will come true, what you told me this past year. Have you been with someone else? Don't lie to me, don't say anything. I know you have been with someone, I saw the stains, you were covered with stains. This is what happens – you are about to tell me, you are dying to tell me, and so you accuse me, you insult me and won't believe that they have put down our wages. I look after you, don't I? It's fine, take me as you want, in the end you always behave the same way, but anyway do get started, even though you wet my whole body. I fall asleep and am not awake to watch over you. I can't follow you all day, can't follow you all day to find out who or what you are thinking about. A gale is blowing between my parted legs, I am freezing inside and you are not there. The night scares me and you take advantage of my fear and tell me that any night you'll go off with some woman or other and now I am frightened that you will carry out your threat. Take me and think about whoever you like, but reassure me until I can feel at ease with the night. Look – I'm lying as you like me. I once knew a boy as frightened as I am. Did I tell you? Are you sure? What I did with that boy he had learned from a dressmaker on the avenue, and that woman had infected him with her fear of the night. We are in complete darkness and I deny myself. I refuse to be tempted by what you offer. I follow, clutching on to you, only so that you can lead me into

the new day, shiny bright like the edge of the coin that
cuts me.

············

I am permanently stricken with pain and fear; an insati-
able hunger devours me. Do you realise that I'm my
head? Don't let them leave me, and don't you leave me.
I'm distraught over my pay and can't manage to make
my way to any office. People are being fired everywhere
you look, and on the eve of my fortieth birthday I shall
be out of a job. It seems as though you are living in
some completely different world, you simply don't
understand what is going on. Exhausted, unemployed, I
let things drift with you since I still have this vague
shifting sense that we are moving upwards. One of these
nights you will end up destroying me, you'll destroy me
for trying to prevent your fluttering flight. You say you
won't leave, you told me you wouldn't, you have even
sworn you wouldn't. But in any case you will finish up
by leaving. Why wouldn't you? All right, go back to join
the others. I was confronted by a flock of hysterical birds
arrested by a copse of felled trees. The birds were
singing a deeply malevolent hymn. You are fed up that
my tongue has lost its dexterity, it's true it isn't easy for
me to take you with my tongue, it seems like yet one
more duty. I'll run my tongue over the length of you,
but don't tell me what you did, don't repeat your story
of the moaning, spare me the details. Don't you realise
that there is nothing? I don't understand what you are
casting around for. There is nothing there. But you carry
on desperately looking, pecking around at the bottom of
things. There is nothing; it just looks like nightfall.
What depths will you resort to? It seems as though you

have just come back from an unlucky journey. Will you come back? A bird departed without warning, leaving me in a state of intense irritation. If you go, someone else will come. At the end of my forties my head is approaching a lethally dangerous zone. Tonight I can see an endless stream of ecstatic bodies, moving so fast that they shatter. Fragments of them fall on me, in the night their splinters shaft me. The final ecstasy echoes in the fastness of your bird's head. What a swindle – for so little I have lost my job, I am separated from the rest of the workers. Concentrating on your shivering, I have become just the shadow of a worker instead of starting a protest march to challenge the slashing of my pay. Opening my eyes I see you, moist. I think you are crying, but I am mistaken – no. You come on top of me and I can scarcely breathe. Someone outside will be waiting for me and a million workers could not protect me when the splinter shafts my eye.

· · · · · · · · · · ·

That night I begged him to help me, for so many years I've been begging him, beseeching him to take away the evil within me, evil that I am. I offered up my sight to make him stop following me, so that he should not always be walking behind me. So many years ago. I didn't want to look, I truly didn't want to look at the boys, suggesting things with my look, nor did I want to feel that moistness – the same as in the film. How moist I became watching the film, it hurt so much that when it was over I could scarcely walk. In those punishing years I needed strength to keep those hands from creeping between my legs to touch me. What pleasure it gave me, I almost came with the man's hand in the park, that man who I thought was deceiving me. Since I didn't know how far his hand would wander, I let him do it, I let him enjoy his own mistake. I didn't have the strength to resist all those hands that tried it, I couldn't cut short my ultimate pleasure. How I loved it when the other man did it to me gently, gently; he touched me so sensitively that when I felt his hand start, when he was starting on me, I stopped him and scratched his hand. Poor man. Don't let it happen to me, don't let it happen, I said, don't let it happen to me again. So I pressed my legs together, sitting on the sofa, until the throbbing began. I wasn't sure, and all I did was to sit on the sofa with my legs firmly together. I should have cut off my hands. I didn't want to see those films that left me afterwards with such an ache, but the man was already following me, aggravating my bad habits and my fear for the safety of my eye. That fear led me to surrender to the hand that sought me out to make me come. But how did I dare tell the man any of this when he showed me how? How could I give it a name and accept it with my own hand? I hadn't learned to bathe myself with the same detachment with which I wash my hands. Once I had overheard the neighbour I would never again be deceived, I understood perfectly what illness it was that she had. It was now that I changed the position of my bed and moved a wardrobe against the wall. I wanted to go to the country, but I might have been attacked by animals. At home I even felt attacked by myself. Everything is dangerous, even a mere film that left me unable to walk. Shopkeepers, craftsmen, bricklayers, carpenters all jostle in my memory like a bird splattered against a window. The world of work marches past before my eyes. The workers are walking in a straight line and their noses are bleeding. I want to bleed, to file past with my fist in the air, yelling for the restitution of our rights, seized by an energy close to hysteria. Bleeding, with my fist held high, I finally understand that wherever I am I am surplus to requirements, that everywhere there lies in wait for me that very thing that made me flee from everywhere.

············

There are three huge birds, black birds perched on the top of a cliff. They sit quite motionless, their beaks raised towards the sun, but they have flown so high there is no warmth. Cheating sun. One of the birds makes a movement and spots me down below in the water. He spreads his wings and swoops down on me with electrifying speed. I shut my eyes and go under. I am going to die. In my dream I am already dead under water and the bird dives down to peck me. The bird is at home on land or at sea. I am waxen and a green stain spreads over my stomach. My corpse keeps a loyal smile on its lips and my lower gum is bleeding from a tiny hole. I've fallen from the top of a cliff and broken my skull, and then the black bird stole one of my eyes.

eight

....

fiesta

In the South Manuel confronted total disintegration. The intense cold pushed its assault to the limit and I had to endure his death rattles at night, that night when an unbearable pain in my side almost paralysed one of my legs. Terrified, I realised that it was a preordained pain, the pressure of which would destroy me. Manuel had gained power over both my physical and my mental future. A number of symmetrical scenes which I badly needed to forget slithered through my mind. When I first knew Manuel someone, more than one person, had already pierced my valiant attempt at dignity. Manuel turned up in the group I used to go around with and I withdrew, feeling at a disadvantage in the face of his obvious difference.

What was it I saw that night? I saw Manuel and felt the release of an overwhelming anguish. My anguish that night found its expression in a horror of misshapen spaces. I must explain it, explain that the line of the street went in a slight curve, and seeing Manuel walking on that crooked street was the first omen. I knew it was impossible to find a way out and was trapped in my own labyrinth.

Manuel leaned, arched against the wall. There was something in his silhouette that I recognised as mine. I was assailed by a kind of mental wailing and had to resort to my familiar escape route. That night I had a mystical experience – I was aware that Manuel had appeared in the icy cold of a long, solemn night. As it was, I felt so uncomfortable with my permanent state of discontent that I had to cut myself off from the group. On my way home I regretted my speechless action, and imagined Manuel going off, furious, through those asymmetrical streets. At this stage my life was ruled by habits of modesty. My wardrobe consisted of one simple dress. As I went along the dress began to cling provocatively to my body. I grew increasingly alarmed and as soon as I got back to my room I undressed to see what on earth was happening to the perverse material. I found nothing, except confirmation that for some strange reason my body had got bigger.

A long time later I would come to understand that Manuel had been detained in the South, and I would get news of his declining condition. I now must stress one detail. The night I met Manuel, the street seemed to go in a slight curve. When I felt my leg going numb, that old street scene came back to me and he reappeared with an arrogance I have rarely seen since. Perhaps I didn't say that Manuel had a large number of phobias and one of his most common fears was that the night, the cold of any night, would destroy him. I understood the root of my sufferings. It was night. My frozen body roused to fury in the night.

· · · · · · · · · · ·

The city was criss-crossed with countless lines of energy. Beams, headlights, lines, circles, traffic jams, these are the makings of a modern labyrinth. Sergio walked through these myriad spaces with admirable precision. Not a sign, not a notice, not a warning perturbed him. His abstracted body took him from place to place. I was mesmerised by his skill and ventured to make a few frozen movements. The city was shrouded in a cloak of hostility. Scared, I confided in Sergio, I told him about the hostility in the city and he looked at me as if he didn't understand a word I was saying.

He gave me to understand that I was crossing a dangerous border; he told me my mind was deceiving me. He explained that death was simply contained within a small part of my own brain.

The cruelty of his statement intensified my condition and sharpened my perceptions. I realised that he wanted to make Manuel disappear from the real world and to stay on himself and puppeteer the man of my desires. He wanted to insinuate his way into my nights to cure his own insomnia. Sergio was sleeping badly and his reddened eyes betrayed the impassivity that he preached. Without paying further attention to his words, I withdrew into my body. Quite unexpectedly I caught sight of my torso reflected in a large shop window in the city and felt a sudden alienation. The image I saw frightened me, since I am exceptionally sensitive to any lack of harmony.

As the months went by I grew disgusted by my body. Between my shoulders and my waist there was an obvious imbalance and I couldn't help being continually tormented by it. Knowing that I must be deformed, I tried to hide the abnormality by dressing in loose, shapeless clothes, but even so the imperfection was detectable. Sergio had already noticed it and suggested that I try a different diet. The evil only attacked in a different place. To be honest I was devouring an excessive quantity of sugar and decided that I must give up sweet things altogether. Thus began another sudden bout of fasting which left me so lethargic that for a while it diminished the danger of other people's bodies.

· · · · · · · · · · ·

I had to recover my figure, to recover my harmony. Lack of food produced various different effects on me. My skin began to be transparent. All my basic needs were reduced, and I wanted to cut them down still further. It was the only way to escape Manuel's calling in the night. My persistent hunger left me only when I slept, and I slept more and more until there were only tiny intervals for Manuel's claims which came with increasing frequency, to the point where they shattered into countless fragments wrapped in white cloths.

It was impossible to verify news that Manuel was in detention in the South with four broken ribs. This explained the bandaged fragments that criss-crossed their way through my nights. I was swollen, broken, misshapen, and my skin was unnaturally transparent. Soon a terrible dryness set in, which I tried to correct by regular intakes of water. That at least got rid of the bothersome flaking which made my skin look dirty from head to foot. I wanted to prevent Manuel with his bandaged fragments from coming back in the middle of the night, when he would press me to make a decision that, through fear and modesty, I found terribly difficult to make. I realised that Manuel's physical condition was the main trap he had set for me. The disgust I felt at my own body increased to the point where I had to reject even the slightest movement towards seeking pleasure in myself.

. . . .

The city held nothing for us. Completely dispossessed, we wandered from one edge of town to the other in pursuit of non-existent jobs. Sergio gave up hope straight away. I, on the other hand, followed up every single lead, burying myself in a disaster zone. I was ready for anything, was prepared to accept the most miserable offer. I wanted to survive, I *had* to survive in the city, just as Ana did, going from one place to the next and thus assuring herself with an ease that I had never known.

Ana tried to persuade me that in the city I was looking in the wrong place; she told me that Manuel had never been rooted anywhere but in the South and what I really couldn't bear was that he had abandoned me. By contrast Sergio undermined me without so much as a look and one of his surest fronts of attack was my body and the changes that he alleged were disfiguring my face. He blamed me for his own incompetence and our lack of funds. I felt overwhelmed by a whole series of subtle pressures and redoubled my efforts to find some source of income. One attack followed another, except for the rare moments when we were radiant with the simple happiness of being unconfined, further and further from the blindly erratic vanishing point.

Someone was following me. I knew quite distinctly that a man was following me as I walked up the avenue. It was already dark and I was walking the streets alone to the sound of music coming from inside the houses. In the midst of traffic I found him. The noise of his footsteps frightened me and when I turned round I could see his shape a little way off. There are no words for the terror I felt, and images were unleashed of death and blindness. An aeroplane overhead broke the sound barrier and the explosion flattened part of the city. I was at the centre of this area and took advantage of the confusion to give the man the slip. He disappeared in the violence of the explosion, leaving me with a curious sense of ambiguity.

· · · · · · · · · · ·

All of a sudden everything happened at once, with various different scenes superimposed, acted out against the backdrop of the vigilant city. I decided to keep the appointment, though I concealed my motives from Ana and Sergio. I had to conquer my fear, I had to suffer the fierce cold, I would have to support myself. The night I arrived at the fiesta, one could glimpse in the cold a faintly murderous atmosphere impossible to control.

Condemned to stay the whole night, I concentrated on observing those perversely painted faces, made up to hide all trace of their true identities. Despite the make-up they were recognisable. There they all were, attempting transformation through the flow of the music. They danced with no grace, their mongrel bodies struggling to force the occasion into a fiesta. Their artificial euphoria made the pretence even more obvious, as did the suspiciously loud music.

Their jewellery jangled against their faces, mainly dark-skinned, their Indian features hardly hidden by their thick hair soaked in sweat. Their cheeks, brightly painted with rouge, seemed completely detached from the rest of their faces. The fiesta had always been a front. There was a crowd of women drawing up the basis of a new constitution. Their thighs were tattooed with symbolic devices. My tattoo burned into the flesh of my thigh. At this fiesta I was initiated as a worker, rejecting the slurs and the bribes they offered me to break the forthcoming strike. Under cover, secretly, I penetrated this world which I'd just joined in order to determine the conditions of victory. I needed to take part in the election of the chief spokeswoman, a beautiful woman, very experienced and a great fighter.

It was a magnificent occasion. They were canvassing for housing, wages and long-term contracts. A giant banner was stretched across the hall which read: 'We'll ensure our demands are known throughout the country, an example to the whole continent which will follow our tattooed women workers, united by the popular emblem etched on their thighs.'

The employees from different federations had reached agreement and the agreement was printed on the banner that they were going to display in the most prominent place on the main avenue. The letters had been drawn by a team of tattooed women and stood out in phosphorescent paint. The confederation had agreed on ten crucial points. The housing problem was one of the ten. A girl read out the document: 'Our bodies bump against walls and the minimum ceiling heights are inadmissible. To protest at this overcrowding we have agreed a demand which is neither conditional nor negotiable. It heads our list of demands, it is the origin of our tattoo, the circled banner of our struggle. The housing problem must be resolved publicly, without any kind of compromise. That is why we have agreed to print these demands on our left thigh and right in the centre of our buttocks. How are we supposed to live if our bodies are cramped up against the walls? How can we go on living like that? We, the tattooed workers, insist our demand for living space is absolutely justified. The country must agree to allow us to live with room enough to breathe.'

No one giggled when the complaint was raised by the provincial federation. I realised that the women saw it as a matter of life or death. Cautiously they began to talk about a general strike since the housing issue allowed no further room for manoeuvre. I decided to oppose both a series of wildcat strikes and direct negotiations with the powerful Federations. One of the workers spoke and I was in raptures over her perfect red fingernails, her thick dark mascara, her beautiful curly wig. We simply must push out the walls and raise the ceilings so we can lift up our heads – it seemed to me imperative. The woman who did the tattoos gave a brilliant explanation of the meaning of her design. I thought it wouldn't hurt to be tattooed, but it did. My skin became slightly infected and I could no longer stand my pants rubbing me.

That night the words 'living space' went round and round in my head until I was obsessed by them. All I wanted to do was to go outside to shout the slogan out loud, to yell it to the crowds. The main speaker was extraordinarily gifted – her election seemed to be in line with her decidedly large figure, the effect of which was heightened by her provocative manner. She thought she was the cat's whiskers. The back-up team voted for a street vigilante gang. I volunteered for training, though I had been too long out of work and had forgotten the terms of my contract. I realised that it was an inevitable fact – nothing was in the least personal while at the same time it all belonged to us. I had attained the conviction that came with my tattoo.

In a strong voice I addressed the meeting, insisting on the importance of the tattoo. The music blared out just as stridently and the main speaker, trained to drown out any noise, could be heard quite clearly. At dawn we were ordered to leave the dance hall. Living space, living space, living space was the slogan.

I went out that morning with the suspicion that I had been the protagonist in a brave dream. That night Manuel made himself felt in the heat of the moment.

···········

These critical conditions, instead of diminishing, spread their roots throughout the city. Sergio spent his time wandering aimlessly without paying attention to the situation we were in. Unconcerned, he spoke only to issue brief instructions about the shortage of supplies, until I finally realised that this situation was the one that suited him best. In it his fears were diffused and his figure lost its oddity. Engrossed in the ambiguity of it all, he was capable of being quite disarming, sowing doubt in the face of all evidence.

Ana started to mistrust him. She told me so openly one evening when I was looking for her, to tell her that I had recent news about what was happening to Manuel. She scarcely listened to what I had to say, but would only speak about Sergio, telling me that I must beware of him since he was bringing part of my life to a close.

I was confused and decided to ask a number of questions. Ana had a marked tendency to lose control and I could tell by the tone of her voice that she was alarmed. When she got into this state I felt I would rather keep well away, guessing that Sergio had hurt her somehow, though without knowing anything definite to confirm my impressions. At the risk of starting a quarrel I asked her to enlarge on her suspicions. It seemed to me that everything she said was very vague, though her animosity towards Sergio was real enough. She looked haggard, as though the tension was strangling her. I realised that her assumptions were the result of exhaustion. A single gesture was enough to let me know how insecure she was, and she told me that she could see how dangerously her room for manoeuvre was closing in on her.

Ana was more resilient than I. She had come to such unshakable conclusions concerning the rest of us that she herself was protected and avoided the focus of attention falling on her. That day her unusual weakness worried me. The real world had got to her and she was on the point of surrendering to its obstacles. If Ana was giving in to exhaustion, I had no alternative but to throw myself into wandering the city, condemned to an existence with no past and no future as a body merely grappling with the primitive act of survival.

I wanted to find a way out and decided to share with her my aversion to depravity. Sergio pleased me at night. His hands explored me beyond all limits. I gave Ana a fairly full description of his behaviour, knowing that it would shake her out of her decline. I spoke to her about depravity. I talked to her at length about how depravity revolted me.

nine

....

knowledge

'What are you doing here?' she asked him.

He didn't answer. He simply looked at her and smiled.

'What are you doing here?' she asked again.

His smile was threatening. She was scared of an explosion and started looking for some means of defence, but guessing in advance that it was pointless she stopped looking round. In any event, he had arrived totally obsessed and nothing was going to hold him back. Francisca could make out traces of decadence in that dangerous, primitive smile and the false exhilaration brought on by strong drugs. She realised that he had taken one of his pills and knew that to be the cause of his air of assurance. There he was before her, dangerous and assured.

She tried to move forward, heading towards the exit. But just as she reached for the door with her hand, 'Don't move,' he said.

She stayed still, watching him. And then she was forced to recognise that she would always stay, that she would never abandon the false perfection of that smile.

'What do you want?' she asked.

'Nothing,' he answered. 'There's something I don't understand. When I've understood it, I'll leave.'

'I don't want you to leave,' she thought. 'Don't go, I shan't let you,' she thought. The charm of his smile had seduced her and she recognised in him the disease that she needed to be able to carry on living. Yet again, she realised, she was about to lie to him. She would tell truly desperate lies now she had seen him so thoroughly animated by his drugs. Corrupted by an energy not her own she felt a sudden compassion. Having dived head-long into compassion, the world closed in around his presence, imbued with an intensity she had always craved.

He carried on, secure in the advantage that his smile assured him, and she realised that nothing made any difference to him now. She saw him as on the verge of unreality and felt she was being consumed by a being that had quite clearly moved on to some other plane. Her compassion vanished as she realised that his smile was nothing but a lie fed by a series of deliberate equivocations, and she shrank back in misery at finding herself part of so fragile an image.

But at the same time the frozen loneliness of that night set in train their ritual touching and a possible way forward opened up for them, so that they were flooded with something akin to the brilliance of the fiesta. The accumulated tension fell from her body and in the delight of relaxation she forgave him the ambiguity of his smile and in so doing even forgave herself.

'Francisca,' he said, 'I can't go on.'

'Yes, you can,' she replied.

··· ·· ·····

(I finished up unbelievably tired. You don't understand, it was because she was dying and if I didn't fantasise she wasn't going to make it through the night. I delayed her dying by a night, by fantasising. 'Stop it, don't keep moving. Why do you always have to keep moving?')

. . . .

It was getting late. The artificial light of the late afternoon marked the inexorable passage from light to dark with a dense reddish coppery ball in a clear sky free from any hint of a storm.

The dull twilight placidly accompanied her to her destination, knowing in advance what she would find once the sun had set, leaving darkness pierced by a single sunbeam, one insistent remnant of the sun lingering in the gloom. She would reach her destination against the backdrop of the chiaroscuro of a cloudless sky, and fervently hoped that the end of her path would not reveal the very sight that had driven her from her house when darkness began to fall.

She was sickened by her own precision, wearied by her habit of meticulousness, and longed to get it wrong and arrive early to avoid the sight; but her mind, fastidious regarding every detail, shortened her stride so that she should arrive at the exact moment of consummation of this rendezvous, at which she herself would only be an intrusion.

Though she realised she was walking towards the very centre of all her stories, victim of a spiteful trap long since laid for her, that afternoon she regretted that the sun did not go mad and plunge down, burning up the earth, instead of quietly and obediently dawdling on its axis.

She knew she was walking straight into humiliation and that she had been expecting this ever since she first learned the meaning of abandonment, and that whatever the meaning of abandonment, it had been ordained long ago, long before she had even been born. She imagined that she was going to confront something cyclical, something that had already happened, which meant that whatever she did it would not be characteristically hers, it would scarcely even be a copy, it would just be one more repetition of the human agenda. She passionately loathed the humility of this repetition, the meagreness of the scope of human conduct. As she went on walking, she passionately loathed herself for facing the chaotic disorder of her emotions every bit as submissively, every bit as obediently, just so she could carry on living in the midst of this destruction. The scorn she felt for herself exploded in violence in the indifferent twilight.

The explosion of her emotions made her lose her memory and she suddenly felt herself to be unique, the one and only victim of an extraordinary story which he had seized to transform into a second story, the point of which she was about to learn. And this is what she was going for – to confirm with her own eyes those images, blurred by her poor sight, that had been etched indelibly upon her memory.

Stripped of even the last traces of pride, stripped of everything she owned, she had resorted to searches, questions, pressures to confirm her own intuitions, which were in fact much stronger than mere intuitions; the host of signs she had accumulated as a result of days and nights of intense concentration.

She was about to arrive at the rendezvous, she was only a few paces away with her heart beating furiously from the uncertainty of what was about to happen, when she felt his eyes on her – mortifying her wasted body.

The mortification was what her body deserved ever since those early days when she had first realised how flawed were her legs, her arms, her waist. Only she knew the full extent of her imperfections and the realisation that her physique could never change filled her with shame and impotence.

In the seconds before the meeting, she pictured in her mind the images she needed to keep her walking forward. She imagined the two of them together. She visualised the first time they had been naked, their hands touching, caressing, coaxing pleasure from the body which until such a short time before had been her own. Her secret imagination lingered on an image of sexual possession. That bastard beneath me, she thought.

She leaned against the wall to light a cigarette and, her mind made up, walked the short remaining stretch. She looked through the windows scanning the tables and saw them at once. She couldn't help smiling. 'At last,' she thought, 'I didn't think this moment would ever come.'

(You can have no idea what it was like to have to listen endlessly to her groaning. For those years my life was permanently riddled with groans. 'Don't look at me like that; don't laugh. Please, don't laugh at me.')

···········

'Don't leave. I promise I won't do it again.'

But he continued, unperturbed, packing his clothes into a bag. 'In my bag,' she thought, and unable to stop herself told him:

'It's my bag.'

He shot her an ironic look then went on, tenser than

before, busy looking things out, choosing things, putting things away. She felt there wasn't enough air. 'I can't breathe,' she thought, 'I'm going to die.' And she couldn't stop thinking how he mustn't go, that she wouldn't let him, that she hated him the more for putting this terrifying pressure on her.

She knew that she must contain herself to contain her hatred, that she must conceal it now to be able to reveal it later, a fraction at a time, in every single one of her actions. 'I must do something,' she thought, without being able to think what. She still hadn't worked it out as he finished his packing and started shutting the bag, deliberately exhibiting himself like the very final image in an apparently definitive last act.

'But it should have been different,' she thought. 'I always thought it would be different.' She already deeply regretted what she had said, speaking as she had, setting an ultimatum, making her words too weighty, beyond the limitations of the screenplay. For a few moments she thought she would do it, but the murderous impulse died and she chose flight instead, to bestow on him a lingering death, a different kind of violence. It would be a death planted in her living body, which had contrived an end he refused to allow her. She was still breathing but she felt as though she was suffocating and as though the asphyxiation itself was now becoming part of her breathing.

Choked by sobs she approached to touch him, but he drew away giving her a warning look. Still choked with sobs she went up to embrace him, moving forward to the kill – each step giving a clear indication of her intention. He shrieked, he almost howled, and came down on top of her and then, much later, he carefully bandaged her with his shirt and dried her with his own trousers.

'I so wanted that,' she said to him.

············

(You can perhaps accept something when you haven't got it before your eyes the whole time. But that's not how it works for me. We seemed to be alone in the whole universe and she was leaving the universe, leaving it in the most heartless way imaginable. 'No, I don't like it like that. I've already told you, not like that – I don't like it.')

············

It was enough for her to avert her gaze to know for certain that something was approaching, but oddly it did not worry her. She was in an unusually calm frame of mind, waiting for him to bring himself to speak. He spun out his words and spun them out as she watched. Gloomily he retraced his useless steps to and fro across the room, getting himself ready, preparing for the right moment.

She prevented her anxiety from gaining the upper hand. A mental block conveniently stifled her momentum and she felt herself rallying to some kind of resistance to that part of him that was preparing to strike the fatal blow.

'She is frightened of me,' he thought,

'He is such a coward,' she thought.

When he said that he was going away for a few days she felt relief to be free from his pacing up and down and didn't feel the need to ask any questions. He is leaving for a few days, she thought. The trap that she herself had set was about to snap under the excessive pressure on one of the springs. She could almost feel her head, her nose, her mouth, making desperate efforts to breathe. Suddenly she was alive, no longer either his prisoner or his warder. 'So, he's leaving for a few days,' she thought; and the journey seemed to her like a kind of truce since she could have a break from the need to spy on him, exhausting herself and exhausting him the whole time.

'So, you're leaving for a few days,' she said to him. 'That's fine by me, absolutely fine.'

He collapsed on to the sofa. He simply let himself drop and he seemed worn out; she saw him as suddenly aged. 'You're tired,' she thought and she felt happy to be sharing something with him, but she was already too bound up in her own coldness to embark on a conversation.

All of a sudden she decided she should go out to avoid coming under attack from her own impulses. She went out in a great rush, even forgetting the formality of a goodbye. Out into the night she went in search of the cold street air, in the hope that the street would bolster her anonymity.

She walked.

Although she knew she had no place to go, or rather that any possible places were only the mirror of her own decline, she allowed her legs to step to the rhythm of the night. She walked on until she was utterly emptied into its disjointed time, branded with the different voices that lived on in her erratic memory. Guided by her need to speak to someone, her walk focused on the urgency of finding a telephone. Finally she managed to get in touch with her from a shop.

'For two hours a man has been following me,' she told her. 'He is as tired as I am. I think he must be worn out.'

She rang off instantly before the other could start raising her voice to that strident tone that so irritated her. She turned back slowly, enjoying the slap of the frozen air on her face and observing the outlines of the houses in the dark, the framework of the windows, the asymmetry of the façades, the diffidence of the thresholds. When she reached her own street she was grateful for the sense of security inspired by being on home ground.

She had only just got into the house when she saw him sitting on the usual sofa and realised that she'd been the victim of a trick. He looked at her as if it was she who had just got back from a long journey; he smiled at her and she was on the point of doing the same, but it was now late at night and night was, in a certain sense, her enemy.

'You're still here,' she said.

'I am waiting for you, Francisca,' he answered her.

············

(In fact I didn't pay much attention. To me, it seemed like something that started from one minute to the next. It started at night – that night I spent with her. With dawn I thought it was ending, that it had been a thing of the dark, but from that moment on her body gave her no respite. I could see the fearful tragedy eating into her body little by little. 'Don't go, listen to me. Why are you always so scared?')

············

He was running his right hand over her face and she was shocked for she had never seen him look so sad, so devastated, as if he had swallowed all the disasters of the world. 'He looks like someone I don't know,' she thought, bewildered, as she let him stroke her. 'It feels like a leave-taking,' her thoughts ran on, but she remained disarmed by his tender melancholy. Nevertheless he gave the impression he would leave, or perhaps what made his gestures seem so decided was in fact nothing more than weariness. 'As if he were tired of me,' she thought, but no one gets tired of someone from one day to the next. She put it to herself that maybe she didn't know him and started to feel overcome with rage at the thought that he had perhaps tricked her far more than she had imagined possible. Though when she watched him so weighed down, she considered it impossible that he would have double-crossed her.

She felt ready to talk, she was about to speak, but he put his hand over her mouth then embraced her, squeezing her so tightly that she could hear his heart beating. In a flash he'd pushed her away and was already in the process of opening the door, even managing a faint smile before leaving the house.

Stunned, she walked across the room and sat down on the chair. She went on staring at the room as if something must have changed, now he had finally left her, but she could find nothing peculiar except that she couldn't put her head in order. It was as if her reason wanted to erase what had just happened.

'I'm cold,' she thought, but as she thought it she knew that wasn't it – she wasn't cold or hungry, she didn't feel anything except an overwhelming desire to stay sitting there for days, for years. 'I could stay here

my whole life,' she thought, leaning her head on the
back of the chair as her eyes closed of their own accord,
overtaken by an irresistible drowsiness. Vague thoughts
struggled to penetrate her mind and she tried to open
her eyes to rid herself of them. When she could see
again, she looked at the room with the eyes of a stranger,
as if the place didn't belong to her. She walked across to
her bed and fell on to it. She lay down and gave herself
over to the bland pleasure of feeling her body stretched
out. She closed her eyes so she wouldn't have the bother
of having to continue her examination of the room, so
she could forget where she was, now she could no longer
share the familiar little space with him. Giving in to the
demands of her body, she stayed lying down and avoided
thinking of what she would do from now on, since any
line of action seemed equally unlikely. She curled up on
her side on the bed longing for the sleep that she feared
would not come, guessing that all she was doing was
putting off the enormity of her solitude.

She was lying lost in oblivion when she heard the
sound of the door. 'He's come back,' she thought, and
was filled with a passionate happiness – though at the
same time she felt tainted by a subtle disappointment.
The man who appeared in the doorway, the man standing in front of her, was the same as ever, despite the fact
that his silhouette was quite dark. She was not surprised
to hear him say, 'All right, tell me everything.'

'It was so good, I couldn't help it,' she answered him.

. . . .

(All at once everything started to revert to normal, as if
reality had been suspended in just one place. Coming
and going, she was weaker each time, contained in the

infinite space of her damaged body. Sometimes she smiled at me. I don't know where she got the strength to look at me and smile. 'Now I'd rather talk. I already told you that I'm in a bad way tonight.')

. . . .

Now he was having fun. 'You're having fun,' she thought. 'You are enjoying my collapse, tonight you are positively enjoying my collapse.' She was beside herself, suffering an illness, infected by the city and the splinters of the city that clung to her body. The city itself was entirely contaminated by an icy virus which ranged freely through its inhabitants; and now he was playing with the disease. He went up to her, took her by the shoulders and steered her into the bedroom. There she allowed herself to be consumed by that particular passion that she could not keep herself from sharing with him. They came together briefly, repeating the best parts of their past love-making, an astonishing exhibitionism of their bodies which used so to dazzle them. Now, by contrast, it seemed like the consummation of a cry whose echo came from some distant place.

The speed of their climax caused her some surprise. As she was getting dressed, she realised that he had lent himself purely in the interests of a renewed attack that would leave her in a wretched state – diminished and pathetic. But her need was paramount and knowing that her desire was greater even than his, she sought him again. No possible law could have held them back. In her acute need she opened doors through which he could vent all his resentments and void the hatred that he had fabricated in his solitude.

Towards the end she tried to avoid the blows and shut

her ears to his words so she could remain focused only on herself. In so doing she achieved an extraordinary descent and wanted to share it with him. As always, she leaned over his convulsive form to take him into her mouth as he begged her to contain each and every spasm. She submitted orally, he was quite out of control and she complied with everything he pleaded for. It was scarcely a truce, more a short interlude of peace achieved through intimacy.

Later she measured the frequency with which darkness caught up with them. She got ready to resist this night, to resist some night or other, protected by an assumed indifference and a complete bodily renunciation. Fleeing her obsession, she closed her eyes and in the shelter of the night, fell into a distressed sleep.

....

(When this happens, words lose all their meaning – or perhaps they don't. Sometimes the two of us latch on to words as if speech could have brought his body's incarnations back to life. 'I know it, tonight you are going to tell me truly dreadful news. It would be better if you told me once and for all what it is you are planning.')

....

They had stopped on the corner and although they knew that people were staring, despite the people, she went on shouting. He was terribly pale and pushed her as he tried to move on. The force of the blow left her motionless, her eyes wide open and her breath cut short. He looked at her without a trace of compassion and continued walking. She stayed stock still exposed to the gaze of the people on the corner, random bystanders who had happened upon a scene they were finding most gratifying.

She overcame her embarrassment and swallowed her sense of pride as she ran after him. As she crossed the street she saw him walking briskly, in a hurry to leave the corner where she had so obviously suffered defeat.

She caught up with him half-way down the block, exactly half-way, and seized his arm. She felt as though she was tottering, on the point of falling over, as if the nerve centre responsible for her sense of balance was damaged. He held her body. She registered as much from the energy in his arm and leaned the more heavily on him, feeling as though it was not she walking along, but a ghost of her former self, her sick and shivering remains, animated only by confused emotion.

On her way home, each step was a torment and gave rise to more and more dire warnings of inexorable judgement. The people who had witnessed her break-down were still there at the corner as she went past, her bowed head inescapably betraying the state she was in. For his part, he said nothing, nor even looked at her, which he thought right, since whatever he had said would have been found wanting, inadequate to describe the sorry state to which she had been reduced.

'I shall not forgive him. This time I am really not going to forgive him,' she thought as she measured mentally how far there was still to go. 'It won't be now, or tomorrow,' she thought. 'It will be later.' And when they got home she went straight to bed. He followed her and stretched out by her side. The mess no longer bothered her. She felt protected by the walls of the room and by the body resting by her side, as though she was beginning to recover and that perhaps nothing serious

had really happened. She observed the progress of the
night as if it could almost embody the indiscriminate
invasion she sensed. Her fear returned at the same
instant as she felt a sudden blow, so effective that for an
instant she wanted to dissolve into the night.

(Throughout this episode I was overwhelmed with
compassion. I would have done anything on earth to
spare her this suffering, but despite the atrocity that
overtook her I could never admit that she should leave
me. Perhaps my mistake was in not letting her die as
soon as she wanted. 'No, tonight I'd like to go out. You
never take me out anywhere.')

···········

This time it was painful. His words succeeded in making
her bones hurt. She felt an intense, merciless pain in
the marrow of her bones. She was bent almost double,
praying that he would go back on his words to cure her
of her sudden affliction. Doubled up, her mental images
proliferated to the very edges of some truthful relationship. She concluded by tying the thread which led to his
frequent absences and to the grim expression he had so
often had on his face at the matchless moments they had
shared. She set up an image of despair and when she
lifted her head it was not she who was looking. It was
someone else.

Part of her body had escaped, the remaining part was
quite without spirit. She realised what she had lost of
herself; all that ran through her now was an irreparable
fragility. She was someone else.

He seemed to be waiting for something, but the truth
was that it wasn't she who was there, it was someone
who had just moved into her body. She felt in need of a

mirror and got up silently to look for her own reflection. There she was, and she smiled to see herself and to confirm that the image she saw was scarcely an imitation. She felt not a flicker of curiosity in front of the face reflected in the mirror. 'It's perfect,' she thought, and felt attracted by its defiant pallor. Her make-believe face took to night in broad daylight, took to morning at night, and having been shown up, longed to forget. She gave in to the necessity of being someone else but could find no words, no images, no thoughts for her.

In the distance she heard him walking about, distantly she heard the warning. At the second crash she realised that he had smashed half her belongings. 'Let him break the lot,' she thought, but registered also that she minded. Each of her things seemed dreadfully important to her. When she got near to him she realised she would have to defend her few possessions.

She surveyed the shattered glass and didn't want to be held up by a cut hand dripping blood. The blood didn't concern her, or the wounded hand. She sensed instinctively that she was going to be knocked down and managed to dodge him. Then it was he who was on the point of falling, and she noticed that he was still holding a splinter of glass in his bleeding hand. Frightened by the sharp edge of the glass, she gave in.

'Let's go to the room,' he said.

She started to walk and broken glass splintered under her weight.

· · · · · · · · · · ·

(Have I told you about the blood? She poured blood from every orifice of her body while I in terror tried to staunch the bleeding with a cloth that she always kept beneath her pillow. 'Never forget your manners. You know perfectly well that the least rudeness bruises me.')

. . . .

My head is bandaged. I open my eyes. My hand moves up to touch my head. It really is bandaged. A little blood is seeping through the bandage and my fingers are red with it. I am dying, dying. The man in the hospital looks furiously at me and shouts at me. I close my eyes. I can still think. My head carries on thinking. Perhaps I'm not dying. But what kind of bandage is this that doesn't stem the bleeding? I need a tighter bandage to stop this bleeding that so appals me. My sight was blurred, worse and worse until I lost sight of the light. I won't open my eyes again, I don't want to know what is going on, I want to block out that shouting. I hate it when they shout, when they shout at me.

In the middle of all this shouting I felt my head split open and my right eye disintegrate. I made a useless attempt to support myself against him so as not to come crashing down. Against the man who wanted to kill me. He split my head in the midst of all this shouting. The bastard wanted to kill me.

'Don't shout at me. Can't you see I've had a terrible fall?'

ten

·······················

gentleness

After selling everything I still possessed, I made my way to the dance hall, thus defending my determination to survive, which I could only do by joining the group at their meeting on the date we'd all agreed. I wanted to recover a sense of ease with my body, so I had enlisted with the workers' shock troops which had drawn up the list of demands.

To avoid suspicion I had to go to the dance that night. It was to be a wild dance, organised mainly to obscure the true subversive purpose of the fiesta. I had put on outrageous make-up – an aggressive shade of red. The red of my lipstick was the same as the flagrant red on my cheeks and enabled me to get my two blackened eyes into line. I had almost had a fit straining to distort them. I concentrated on details that I had never thought of till then, like the way my arms were covered in closely woven elasticated fabric to protect me from any rough contact on the dance floor. I knew that the dance could end in violence – the sense of pressure was unmistakable and we were already too vulnerable and exposed.

The dance that night was an occasion that attracted the hungry, and hunger could at any moment set off a catastrophe. The make-up was there to diminish the dangers of animosity.

After two or three hours dancing I was no longer sure if my body was still my own. Sweat had ruined all our cosmetic efforts and turned us into weird apparitions. I began to recognise a few faces and to catch the drift of some of the conversations. 'Remember?' 'Do you remember?' was the phrase I heard most, repeated in an attempt to sum up the nostalgic confusion over the importance of work and working conditions. I overheard, 'You're the same as the night (*perhaps your head has been turned and you no longer know what's happening*) without having a clue as to what was going on. How come you didn't know they were getting rid of the workers? I told you often enough, don't you remember?'

Suddenly the scene shifted and the start of the meeting was announced. The assembly listened to a rapid series of personal accounts:

'I said I wasn't at peace and it was true. I've always felt I have to be on my guard in the dark. I was convinced it was my thoughts that were wrong. I really tortured myself about it. Don't you remember?'

'And it was my patience that you took advantage of to carry on abusing me. You abused me terribly, don't you remember?'

Delegates from all over the country paid attention to these stories which set the context in which to frame their demands. Only one faction remained dubious, insisting that it was essential to present the petitions gradually. The delegate from this faction spoke in favour of a longer timescale, backing her arguments with historical allusions, speaking of tactics and strategies. Her faction wanted to broaden the scope of the agreements and to defuse the possibility of street riots. It favoured discussion and was against a general strike. The delegate outlined an organisational plan that would cause confusion and delay. Another girl accused them of being wildly over-simplistic in their ideas of good and evil and tabled a vote of censure for trying to split the party.

The meeting had already lasted nine hours through the night, and those nine hours had taken their toll on the fine rhetoric; by now everyone was keen to hurry the proceedings on to the final resolution. It was essential to offer some kind of truce to those impenetrable and mainly taciturn faces. In that sea of unfathomable expressions I was arrested by one face which wore an absolutely fixed expression. It belonged to a young girl, fresh from the country, who followed the debate moving her body as if she was listening to a secret song. She looked like a dancer wearing a ceremonial mask. The young worker had nails bitten to the quick and her shoulders were deformed by a severe curvature of the spine. Someone put an arm round her and the girl winced with pain and put her hand to her waist. It was an unforgettable vignette.

The rebel faction kept up their disagreement and were on the point of abstaining altogether. They conspired and talked among themselves with definite gestures and expressions of contempt. A delegate from the textile industry asked them to sign the agreements. The faction, through their spokeswoman, indicated that they had no mandate to decide anything that night. I felt vitiated by the feebleness of the statutes and could see how enforced labour ethics might crumble. There would be no agreement tonight, or on any subsequent night. The workers had been infiltrated even in their own minds. There would be no agreement. There would just be a failed dance, make-up, and the parody of speechifying.

Yet again I had made the mistake of believing a bastard worker's dream. I understood the solitude that awaited me and the necessity of accepting a fixed salary which would be my lot till I died – a miserable end for a miserable wage, which was all a job of mine was worth. A hired hand hidden in imaginary flight. I had sold everything I possessed to get to the workers' assembly, but the workers had been badly infiltrated. They were dependent on a salary they could only dream of – the reduced pay for bodies that had to dance till death – which rewarded the marginal, the factions, the primitive hatred of noble gestures. My reward was one anarchic word, a groan in the night, a pointless demand. I would have to live in abject conditions, vulnerable to the realities of the flock. My only job was to survive in austerity, swallowed up in the city centre.

············

My hopes were shattered, and I was leaning against the wall of a bar when Ana and Sergio came back to me for the last time. They had come back, and I remember needing them then as at no other moment in my life. But on their return they were utterly devoid of expression and stripped of all their power. Sergio seemed scarcely even a feeble pretence, someone alienated by the incomprehensible way his life story had been squandered. Ana also seemed confused. I had built the two of them up and taken them apart again in the course of a drunken session in which I made them the centre of a fantasy I was living out in a dimly lit bar.

I haven't mentioned in my account that Sergio and Ana were lovers, I didn't mention it until now for fear of highlighting the way in which they were struggling to attain a tragic destiny. It was their common unhappiness that was the real bond which kept them in that alarming relationship. It was a giddy relationship that needed them constantly to change their habits as they ran through the range of their resources.

Sergio and Ana had known each other almost since childhood and from then on they started on a strained pursuit of brutal experimentation. The experiments were designed purely to test the limits of the resistance of their bodies. If I speak of brutality, it's because it's the word that best describes the rarified atmosphere they moved in. They were committed to an impossible enterprise – to completely void the other in order to attain self-liberation. Though I can't swear to it, in fact I'm still not absolutely certain that it was liberation they were seeking; despite my constant surveillance I could not break into the secret world that existed between them. The two of them had some cryptic communication, and that mystery was the root of the power they had over me.

I haven't mentioned how they captivated me, nor have I said how badly I wanted to take possession of their minds so that I could take part in their uninterrupted fiesta, join in the timeless dance that held them in a state of perpetual ecstasy. I realise that I've used a rather trivial phrase, 'perpetual ecstasy', a phrase that might give a false picture of them. If I've settled on the word 'ecstasy' it is to emphasise the lethal aspect of this relationship, a destructive force that, without ever being consummated, was for ever on the point of consummation.

Though I realise that any description is vitiated by ambiguity, I prefer not to betray my own feelings because it was precisely my feelings that attracted me to their bodies. I have to say, however, that their bodies overall were pretty insignificant, as insignificant as their manners and their thoughts. They were neither beautiful nor clever and they didn't even consider the possibility of cultivating their intelligence, only acquiring a certain majesty when they advanced on to moral ground – an area by its very nature closed off by impossibility, an impossibility cursed by its dangerous border with probability. But it remained an impossibility, and I knew it, I was so convinced of it that I could never explain the truth of it. I was afraid that if I let the insurmountability of this barrier show, they would come to seem worthless and their insignificance would drag them into a life that, though livable, would in the end not be worth living.

I have already said how much they captivated me, so intensely in fact that they started playing a major role in my own life. I was utterly incapable of distancing myself from them and was a passionate witness to their every movement. I wouldn't dare to describe them as desperate movements, since every desperate move is deliberately obscene, but they certainly were excessive moves, in fact so excessive that I often felt the urge to restrain them. But I found the courage to realise that if I did that, I would only be acting out of my own everyday sense of emptiness. So I held back, even though I knew that together they were balanced between life and death, I mean they were actually playing with life and death – but in their game there was a deep sense of humanity, such a fierce disconcerting attachment to being human that they were transformed in my sight into creatures quite sublime.

None the less I have to admit that they could also seem quite repulsive, as so often manifestations of humanity tend to repel me. I know that my passion for them would be quite incomprehensible without admitting the disgust they so frequently inspired. I am talking of disgust in the context of an intolerable situation, a sense of unexpected death that attacks me when things intangible turn tangible before my eyes. I find, for example, sweaty bodies or aseptic bodies equally disgusting. I loathe, with equal intensity, the pathetic demonstration of pain or any triumphant gesture of delight. What disgusted me about those two was their all-embracing closeness that often meant you could not tell them apart. Their physical closeness was devoid of all sensuality and focused solely on attaining an absolute correlation between their minds and their bodies. This primitive obsession was utterly anarchic, and I stayed aloof for fear of being dragged into the same moral morass in which the two of them seemed perpetually agonised.

My feeling of disgust evaporated when I watched them involved in fierce hostilities. Though this was equally primitive it was at least full of curious subtle sensuality.

Although this sensuality was closely linked to death, I nevertheless felt it contained a kind of generosity in the dazzling display of desire that ranged over the entire surface of their bodies.

Their desire was exorbitant, a force that whirled wildly in all directions, and because of it I could, as never before, absorb the predicament of their bodies. I could understand the redeeming power – magnificent and painful – of being human; I mean the finite sign of the perilous death of desire. Their desire was doomed to die a death that they refused to accept. They were determinedly stubborn and withdrew to the very edge of reality, to a zone where they could act out their fantasy, opening up a space where their desire could survive, could nourish them, could lead them to the validation of their dancing bodies which, however devastated, still shattered any gentleness.

I was seduced and, most of the time, infected by the ferocity to which they rallied them, I was so obsessed that I failed to look after my own physical condition. Nothing was left of myself, not even my desires were my own, perhaps because they had been obliterated for so long. All I had left were Ana and Sergio's desires and I hated both of them for condemning me to a dispossessed existence. I am forced to admit I worried that my hatred would actually destroy their shameless sense of being human; as I've already said, if they'd lost their humanity, their decadence would have become apparent, putting them on a level with the majority of people – placid and insignificant.

But it was in the character of my hatred that I was eager for them to survive the different stages and I hoped their inevitable icy fall would not utterly crush them. When they collapsed, at the very point when they were finally overcome by exhaustion, I felt such a piercing pain that for a moment I lost consciousness. Their collapse actually became a part of me – the part that refused to accept the separation between probability and impossibility. Ana surrendered. Sergio had the upper hand and it was Ana who suffered the full effects of the blow that he so skilfully administered. I suffered Ana's defeat; she and I both lost our balance and we fell together. Ana and I were both struck down by Sergio's hand, a subversive force infiltrated into every nook and cranny that had made survival possible.

The night, the night's darkness and blood were hardly even feeble allies. Sergio would set off along his well-trodden path and Ana too would take her familiar route. Sitting at a table in the ill-lit bar, the tragic sense of my own destruction came home to me when I saw my hand moving to pick up the glass. As I picked it up, Ana and Sergio were completely discarded.

· · · · · · · · · · ·

I was no longer bleeding. I knew I had stopped bleeding when I gave up expecting it to start. I wasn't expecting it since the flow of blood didn't affect me with even the slightest sense of amazement. I was definitely bleeding, I went on bleeding, but only as a physical duty, the imposition of a completely futile biological repetition. Out of inertia and in response to the monotonous signal, I had become like all other bodies, obliged to reveal the evidence of a wound, the price of an immemorial birth.

Blood had become transformed into a neutral liquid that caused me only routine annoyance and ruined a few of my days. I was no longer bleeding. When I stopped even feeling surprised, I realised the scant importance of my body. It was simply matter under stress, on which were woven the threads of a story leading inexorably to an agonising end. I knew the body in agony, I had seen it decompose before my eyes. The agony had lodged in my limbs and the flow of blood had successfully distracted me from it. But now I was no longer bleeding I had to discover what were the true possibilities of my story, how I could construct my farce of a story.

It was fitting for me to live in a space with no history,

on barren ground, in relentless pursuit of a gathering of
minds. I had the vivid impression that I completely
lacked any goal and decided to make my last move. I
made the decision knowing perfectly well that I was
running the risk of hitting very bad weather. In my mind
I sketched out the idea of the journey. I would travel
South and I invested what remained of my strength into
making the journey South.

············

I embarked on the journey. When I started out I didn't
take into account the length of the route, still less the
complications of the country. As I travelled South,
nothing I saw managed to capture my attention, I was
going solely to check whether Manuel still existed,
whether indeed he had ever existed. The South
amounted to no more than an empty word signifying the
position of a putative body and respite from the insecurity of my life. I was confronted by a completely alien
landscape which nevertheless didn't seem at all unfam-
iliar. There I was. I had arrived at the end of an absurd
pilgrimage whose destination I didn't even know. In my
confusion I had reached the depths of the South,
deposited somewhere entirely without significance.

After so many hours on the road, everything began to
look the same and my vague points of reference were
wiped out. I was completely disorientated when I
remembered Pucatrihue. I don't even know what sign-
posts there were to enable me to find the complex route
between their tightening hold and my own fear.

The terror started in Pucatrihue. My anxiety was
provoked by a distressing vision. The fact that I was in
work was just the chance to touch a starving half-blind

bird that left the flock as it made its escape from
Pucatrihue to warmer climates where it could survive
the icy conditions that were drawing in.

It was startling to observe them crossing the sky in
their tyrannical formation, to see them attacking the sky
with their wings. On this occasion I remember the birds
were quite open about letting themselves be seen. They
allowed themselves this display from their conviction
that their flock was impregnable, a single body fanning
out in monstrous movement, etching nightmare images
on the sky – an appalling black cloak shrouding the
evening sky with terrible omens. A nightmare sky, a
despairing flight, I remember, was all I managed to
decipher with eyes that became inflamed as I realised
the meaning of this absolute blackness under which they
hid their sinister intent. I remember that a sudden
question occurred to me: how to escape my own death;
while at the same time my admiration grew for the
magnificent physical exercise of these birds in search of
warmth.

I recognised a ferocious will to live in them, one that
broke every pattern. The supreme spectacle being
played out before my eyes was simply the enactment of
the will to live. It was a savage scene in which the birds
sealed their indissoluble pact. An implacable will to
harmonise their luxuriously spread wings, ever more
widely extended, throbbing with anguish.

I was terrified, I remember, at the recognition of an
extravagant, fanatical intelligence in this black mass, a
fundamental intelligence alert to the onset of the cold
that we others would have to endure. They, by contrast,
were leaving their histories behind, directed by a physical drive that had warned them of the danger. I had

never before seen a group at once so many and so hierarchical, a group that in defiance of risk would take so definite a course. The birds, I remember, were singing in the sky, they were screeching, though what it was that so delighted them I could not tell. They were migrating, screeching with happiness or with pride or with panic, all singing different tunes – it was, none the less, harmonious, one of those contemporary harmonies where every solo is in fact carefully orchestrated.

Above all the squawks were of pleasure, a guttural, savage pleasure that put things human to shame. The sound rolled on to burst into another equally unexpected rhythm. At one stage I remember looking at them with resentment for the incredible impunity of their flight, for the cold indifference of their wings, for the selfishness spread by their song. I remember well, as I watched them, the resentment I felt at the cold that gripped me, helplessly following them with my gaze across the sky. In my resentment I recognised the murderous intent of their flight. The birds would do absolutely anything to survive and this was why they sang, this was the reason for the primitive barbarity that possessed them. The birds like parasites fed only on warmth, and lack of warmth drove them mad. The flock was criminal, it was obsessive; and it withdrew in line with the horizon of my right eye, splitting my retina. I was terribly upset, I remember, and realised that the birds were enraged by the changing seasons and that as for me, I belonged to a frozen region that condemned me to a frigid fate.

I remember well that I couldn't help feeling surprised at my discovery as the birds continued their flight overhead. I wanted to be sure that I wasn't just the victim of an unfortunate suspicion and with my impaired vision – I have already said that I had partially lost my sight, the sight in one of my eyes – I watched them trailing the symptoms of a progressive disease, confirmation that my journey was without significance.

The South was nothing more than that ominous flight of birds, shining behind my back like a sharp weapon ready to rip apart any obstacle in its path. I blamed myself, I remember, for the delusion that had led me to believe that I had some kind of guarantee of physical safety. The South had wrecked my confidence by making clear to me the futility of the pleasure I took in my filament of blood, a delight I could never share. In my head I heard the screeching of the birds, a paradox, I realised that I had never before heard a fuller, more unambiguous sound. This loud, public screeching was so absolutely justified that the cowardly flight of the birds was transformed into an epic of deliverance.

It was at that very moment, I remember it well, that I decided to go back to my place of origin. Without any clear idea as to where my place of origin might be, I set off on an exhausting march towards the anonymity of the centre. I well remember that march, it was utterly resigned, stripped of any trace of vain hope. As I was crossing what I have called the South, the flocks of birds followed in flight behind me, heightening the crisis at hand. A huge blind eye obscured the horizon and an implacable cavity in my brain unbalanced my steps towards the centre.

With my clouded sight, I saw I was in charge of a paralysed animal on the point of collapse. I realised that nothing I had counted on had ever really existed and that I had simply invented a combination of names to counter the birds' flight and to write a history for myself that would soon be legible. I understood, I remember, that empty spaces and flocks of birds were the only realities and that the flocks dominated everything with the speed of their demands. As my vision faded so did my pride and I realised once and for all that I was nothing more than a mouth consumed by the clamour of the city centre.

eleven

....

When I lifted my head I realised what it was about them that I had to write. I was rather depressed to realise how far down a risky path I'd already gone, but knew I had to carry on, since my heart was frozen and urgently needed a little warmth.

I began the agonising journey of retracing my own steps, decoding the hieroglyphics on the fringes of my mind. I'd thrown out the ideas that would have been the most help and had fallen back into a history whose course was exceedingly dangerous.

As I buried myself in the writing, the mental images all began to condense into such chaotic forms that I was almost forced to give up any attempt at creating a comprehensible shape. I had agreed to weave together very exactly all the different threads of the fiesta to create the illusion of a real plot. I tried to impose on it a logic, but it was riddled throughout with outside sensations which so interfered with the edges of my mind that in the end I simply stopped everything else and concentrated only on my current situation, ignoring the monotony and the absence of events that would allow me to distinguish between different periods of my story.

Exasperated, I tried to find techniques, *formulae in the process of failing, to thereby negate that space where the payment of debts crosses over into inflicting wounds in those areas of greatest vulnerability.* I stayed shut in my room most of the time, waiting to be calm enough to recover from the exhaustion of the journey. I no longer had palpitations – my heart was beating quite normally. It was such a long time since I had been without heart trouble that I felt that for once I could not help oversleeping. Half asleep and quite hopeless, I let myself be drawn into a void where they appeared fleetingly, flying past without their hierarchical formation.

But it didn't turn out like that. One night I got up, my feelings in turmoil, and realised my own persistence *could contain each one of the floodgates.* I would write about them from the lonely safety of a room in my house. I got up in the pitch dark and looked for the proofs I'd kept. There were the tapes, the letters, the photographs. There we were, captured in a boxful of artefacts; I immediately set to to catalogue them with my all too familiar obsession.